Vol. 13

Also by Jon Konrath

Fiction:

The Failure Cascade (2020)

Ranch: The Musical (2019)

Book of Dreams (2018)

Help Me Find My Car Keys And We Can Drive Out! (2017)

He (2015)

The Memory Hunter (2014)

Atmospheres (2014)

Thunderbird (2013)

Sleep Has No Master (2012)

The Earworm Inception (2012)

Fistful of Pizza (2011)

Rumored to Exist (2002)

Summer Rain (2000)

Nonfiction:

The Necrokonicon (2006)

Dealer Wins (2004)

Tell Me a Story About the Devil (2003)

Vol. 13

Jon Konrath

"Sleep Letter Zero," "Someday This Could Be You," and "Chili Sweats at Aerie #666" first appeared in *Mandatory Laxative* #14.

"The Metaphor of Poundcake" first appeared in *Horror, Sleaze, and Trash.*

"An Open Letter to S.C. Johnson and Son, A Family Company" first appeared in *The Strange Edge Magazine* Issue Zero.

Paragraph Line Books
Oakland, CA
http://www.paragraphline.com

For more information, please visit
http://www.rumored.com

ISBN: 978-1-942086-07-9

PL-119 (v2)

Fuck Olives

So I was at this party in the basement of a bombed-out, pre-gentrification Williamsburg brownstone. It looked like the underground, post-apocalyptic hideout of the resistance fighters from a *Terminator* movie, but without any cool laser guns. Williamsburg was still a hellhole then; no baby strollers, vegan cupcake bakeries, or dog cafes. It was all vacant lots, cars on fire, *Do the Right Thing*-looking bodegas, and people shooting two-dollar heroin into their eyes. This was back when Bernie Goetz unloaded a revolver in some muggers' faces, and everyone's reaction was like, "Eh, whatever."

The party was for the release of the newest issue of some friend of a friend's zine. Once again, dating myself — this was when people photocopied zines and sold them at record shops and the backs of weird indie book stores that smelled like incense and dust mites. (Back when there were record shops and book stores. And when people still read.) This guy everyone called Brutal Peter did a zine about crust punk music and bass fishing, and I don't care about either, but there was supposed to be free food, so what the hell.

I was trying to flip through this photocopied thing about how pro angler Jimmy Houston was total fucking anarchy, and Ralph Nader cornered me in a kitchen, telling me about how he thought the first two Darkthrone albums were the

only good ones, and they sold out after that, which is ludi-
crous, because *Under a Funeral Moon* is like the best fucking
album ever made, and their first two were like Entombed
ripoffs, before they even got into black metal. I don't know
why Nader was there; probably because there was free food. I
don't know if he was into bass fishing. I tried to ask, but he
thought I said "bass fisting" and started laughing until pieces
of Doritos goo shot out of his nose.

I know it's cliché and everyone in the scene has a story
about getting stuck in an endless black metal conversation
with Ralph Nader, who is very vocal about correcting people
about things that are his own opinion and are generally
completely wrong. One time I ended up with him at the
Feast of San Gennaro street fair. I was supposed to meet
with Anderson Cooper to buy illegal fireworks, and Nader
tagged along, but then Cooper ditched both of us to go eat
at Adrien Brody's new *The Pianist*-themed restaurant in
Times Square. (I won't go into the details of why this was
such a horrible idea for a restaurant, and offer the unrelated
criticism that you shouldn't offer RC cola as your only soda
option. I understand times are tough and running a restaurant in Manhattan isn't cheap, but stick to Coke or Pepsi
products, preferably Coke.)

The Cooper ghosting left me stuck with Ralph, so we
went looking for cheap corn dogs and that dude who used to
sell cheap ZZ Top bootlegs at street fairs. Nader spent the
whole time trying to convince me *Wolverine Blues* was the

best metal album of 1996, which is doubly wrong, considering one, it sucked shit, and two, it actually came out in 1994. And we never found the corn dogs or the bootlegs.

Years later, I was in this Brooklyn basement, trying to read this zine, and half-listening to him babble on about how bad all the Norwegian band's albums on Moonfog records were, and calling it Moonfrog records, and I could barely hear him because someone was playing an early Extreme Noise Terror album on a Radio Shack record player that must have cost $8 back in 1977, and it was dark because the entire basement was lit by a single 40-watt bulb. And there was a bunch of food on the table, mostly generic breakfast cereal and bowls of tapas stolen from some cheap Pakistani restaurant where cab drivers eat and use the toilet between fares.

The stress-shame-eating reflex kicked in, and I started shoveling whatever was on the table in my mouth without looking, and I think one of the bowls was olives. And I hate olives. Seriously, fuck olives. I think part of it was back in high school, I was breaking apart this imitation Strat Jimi-style in my mom's kitchen, and I knocked over a five-gallon glass jar of olives, and my asshole alcoholic stepdad held a gun to my head and made me eat all the olives off the floor, and I swallowed a bunch of broken glass too, which was probably better than the olives.

That asshole later died in a pool of his own blood, shot in the face and balls 27 times by a white supremacist high on crank who got into an argument with him about the 2004 White Sox, which should have made me happy, but of course it doesn't work that way. His death was long after he left my life, but I never forgot the olive incident, a hundred thousand dollars of therapy later. So fuck olives. (And fuck Juan Uribe, who left the Rockies for the White Sox in '04, and all of his stats like doubled – his offensive wins above replacement went from 0.6 to 2.8 after he got done gold-bricking in Colorado.)

I was starving, and Nader wouldn't shut up about how cool it was that Darkthrone's drummer used the name Hank Amarillo for their first album, and I started shoveling down these fermented vegetables without thinking about it. But once I had three handfuls in my mouth, I realized they weren't olives – I was really eating a plate of human eyeballs, covered in an olive oil sauce. A buddy of Brutal Peter's who contributed to the zine worked as a prop master on one of the *Law and Order* shows, and had a hookup with a pathology lab, so he pickled spare ocular organs in his basement apartment. It was one of those hipster artisanal operations that was probably a breeding ground for anthrax, way before anthrax was cool. I spit eyeball chunks all over Nader, ran out of the basement, and spent the next three hours trying to catch a bus back to Queens.

I hid in a bus shelter, puking eyeballs, thinking of a time a few years ago when I used to kinda-sorta date this woman in Stamford, Connecticut. It took me three hours to visit her: two subway lines, two buses, three transfers with those crappy little paper tickets that don't work half the time, 45 minutes of waiting in the cold, and a walk of a mile and a half. I had a car, or an excuse of a car, an old Volkswagen Rabbit that broke down every other time I drove it. I seldom took the VW up there, because it took even longer than mass transit, and I didn't want to get stuck on the 95 with an engine fire. I didn't even want to visit her most of the time, but Connecticut had some nice malls, and I loved going to malls for some sick reason, the same reason people listen to country music or put boards up their asses. When you live in extreme pain, sometimes you need even more pain to feel alive. Also, there was this really slutty chick that worked at the American Eagle Outfitter's at Danbury Fair Mall, and I always wanted to see if she was wearing a bra.

On my last trip to Stamford, the only other person on the bus was listening to a solo album of one of the guys from Dokken, or maybe Winger; it was full of horrible guitar solos and someone yelling "Woo! Woo! Woo!" like if Sammy Hagar played Rick Flair in a made-for-TV movie. The kid wore really old Walkman headphones, the kind with orange foam earpieces that only got about 40% of the sound into the wearer's ear canal, echoing the rest through the bus. I wanted to slam his head into the unpadded metal seat frame fifty times and throw the tape player into traffic, but the windows on the aging GMC didn't open. I hoped eventually his batteries would run out, or the country would get hit by a rogue North Korean test missile and we'd all get killed.

It seemed counter-intuitive to go to the mall and spend my last $37 on discount Halloween costumes and cut-out tapes at the dollar store. I wasn't even seeing her; I had a disabled car parked at her place and needed to get it out of there ASAP. She was in Toronto, fucking a guy who got her free baseball tickets in the nosebleed section of the Rogers Center to watch a forgettable game against the Tampa Bay Jesus Rays. I knew the relationship was over when she wouldn't stop talking about the Blue Jays, socialized health care and maple syrup. I knew the car was over when pouring brake fluid in the master cylinder was like dumping water in the top of a Mr. Coffee with no pot below it. I got two quarts of Prestone DOT 3 all over her apartment parking lot before the Armenian maintenance guy came out, threatened to beat the shit out of me with a tire iron, then told me about the chick's infidelities.

I walked to a nearby Rite-Aid to use the pay phone and leave her sixteen messages on her home answering machine, like a delayed-action time bomb that would eventually explode when she got back to Toronto. I then tried to kill myself with Benadryl and Fiber One bars, which didn't do much except make me hallucinate about the death of Brandon Lee and the NTSB facility in Ashburn, Virginia where they keep the wreckage of TWA Flight 800. I gave up on the suicide solution and caught a bus to the mall.

The bus driver pulled into the parking lot of an Osco drug store, which was a tell for me that this was all a bad dream or allergy medicine hallucination, because there were no Oscos this far east. It was like the time I walked across the George Washington Bridge in a thunderstorm to Fort Lee, New Jersey and found a Kroger's that sold every discontinued White Castle sandwich in the freezer section. I think the thunderstorm killed me, and all this took place in that weird DMT-release pre-death state you hear so much about from ayahuasca enthusiasts with too much time on their hands. I woke up, checking my teeth for the usual dream dental trauma that didn't happen, then chugged a gallon of V-8 fruit juice along with a few Ambien, which would later cause me to shit the bed.

The bus driver — or the dream apparition of a bus driver — told us he had a 15-minute union-mandated break and he was going to go inside and shoot heroin in the restroom, so we had to get out of the bus so he could lock it up. The Osco was connected to a Jewel grocery (they were two different entities though, two sets of cash registers — you couldn't take stuff from the Osco and pay for it in the Jewel, so what's the point really), and I considered going in there for the Halloween candy, but I somehow knew it had a fundamentalist Christian manager who didn't believe in Satanic holidays and refused to stock anything but Jesus Bites, these horrible sugar-free candies made out of olives or dates or some other natural sweetener bullshit. I went into the drug store to make fun of the prepaid Android phones and window-shop the various enema products.

Hours later, the bus driver overdosed in the men's room, dropper in arm, pants around his ankles, and the store security guard pulled out his vomit-covered corpse, threw it on the floor in the candy bar aisle and pissed on him to revive him, moaning as his muriatic output shot onto the man's face and dribbled all over his bus driver uniform vest.

"Why are you doing that? I think that only works for jellyfish stings," said a geriatric woman with one of those wire old lady grocery push-carts, filled with 39-cent tins of dog food she bought to eat with her Social Security check. The janitor kept pissing anyway. Pissing is like eating Jays potato chips: once you start, you can't stop.

A decade later, and it took three hours to catch a bus home from Brooklyn, because the G train is bullshit and doesn't work. The eyes I ate had a horrible aftertaste, and I was still pissed off at Ralph Nader for insisting that Entombed used a Japanese Boss MT-2 Metal Zone pedal for their signature sound, when everyone knows they used a HM-2 Heavy Metal distortion. By the time I got to my apartment a half-day later, I had 23 phone messages from Nader telling me about how he was going to start an extreme noise band called Unsafe at Any Speed and he needed to borrow my Korg M1 synthesizer. And I couldn't stop thinking about that girl, so much so that I couldn't jerk off for a week. Also, fuck olives.

Mariah Carey Is Punk as Fuck

I met the Craigslist guy in a rock and roll McDonald's, one of those fake-ass plastic Fifties versions of the franchise with chrome everything and a set of booths built into a fiberglass replica of a T-Bird convertible. The restaurant had the same garbage food as the other billions and billions of locations, but they piped in sanitized Fifties beach music to make the old people happy. The meeting location was his idea; I would have rather met at a police station or nudie bar, but fried food is fried food.

His ad stated he could give me access to a portal into another dimension and escape this world of shit in exchange for a near-mint GameBoy Color and the *Empire Strikes Back* cartridge. (That wasn't the cool version done in vector graphics where you blow up the Death Star; it was a crappy side-scroller that looked like *Mario Brothers* but with Tauntauns.) I figured any other dimension had to be better than the current one, and I needed answers, meaning, something. And the Game Boy was just sitting in the closet, along with the other thousand pieces of obsolete technology I bought off eBay to make my life complete, which didn't.

"I was hanging out with Al Jourgensen from Ministry at a Hooters and drinking Bartles & Jaymes wine coolers before I came over here." He carried a backgammon set in a wooden box, and smelled like cheap cigars and Aqua Velva. "You play?" he asked, shaking the box. "I got addicted to the one on Windows, kept uninstalling it, but the damn thing kept coming back. I like to play hobos for money, try to bet them their souls, like that Chuck Daniels song about the fiddle. I done told you once you son of a bitch I'm the best there's ever been."

I tuned out his babbling conversation, uninterested in his stories about board games, bad alcohol, and old industrial music. The dizzying sentimentality of the fake nostalgia backdrop somehow made me temporarily obsessed with distant memories of the fabled McPizza, which I'd never seen in the wild. Every time I thought about ordering the pizza back in the 90s, I didn't — alcoholic blackout, food poisoning, terminator robot attack, etc. Now, it was only available at the Pomeroy, Ohio McDonald's, which oddly enough was also the home of Ambrose Bierce. (I think his disappearance has something to do with the limited availability of the McPizza. Maybe they both vanished for the same reason. Aliens, probably.) I heard rumors that the rock and roll McDonald's still had pizzas. This one didn't, but maybe it was a secret menu item, and I needed to order combinations of everything else until I got the pizza.

I didn't care about pizza, and didn't want to eat a pizza, but now I *needed* the pizza. I'd already eaten 4000 calories of fried garbage, but I had to fuck one of those McPizzas. I almost thought about booking a trip to Pomeroy, a town of 1,800 people on the Ohio river, where the fanciest restaurant is a Long John Silver's and the closest airport is probably the one in Columbus, a hundred miles away. So no direct flights — maybe I could take a puddle-jumper to Athens, but it probably stops in Columbus first, so it would be easier to rent a car and drive. And I'd have to make sure to rent an American car, so some deranged ex-coal miner with black lung psychosis didn't beat the shit out of me in a Taco Bell parking lot because I was in a Hyundai, and remember Pearl fucking Harbor.

While the dude rambled on about why wine coolers were awesome, I thought about every pizza I've ever eaten, from birth to present: frozen pizza; pizza-in-a-box kits; Pizza Hut; Pizza Ass; Pizza Pizza, unbaked take-out pizza; dessert pizza; breakfast pizza; Lunchables pizza; astronaut pizza; Chicago pizza; no-real-pizza-is-thin-slice-New-York-pizza, fuck-your-deep-dish-Chicago-pizza pizza; no-fuck-your-thin-sliced-greasy-shit-pizza-Chicago-is-real-pizza-pizza. Do you ever learn to eat pizza, or is it instinct? They used to give us "Mexican pizza" in school, little hexagons of microwaved shit and hamburger meat, or the standard cold, greasy rectangles, like an American flag of lard, with no stars and stripes. Salute the flag, stand upright at attention, because every artery has hardened from cholesterol. "One nation, under gout..." Cut that Mexican pizza into a pentagram. Hail Satan. Build a pizza wall, make Pepsi pay for it.

And then I drifted to a night in the summer of 1992, listening to Mariah Carey's second album *Emotions*, vomiting Papa John's through my nose. Never again, I must forget the garlic butter-topped pizza of that Carrot Top-faced freak and his big-headed NFL life companion, hawking cheap pizza to people with no health insurance. "And lead us not into temptation..." I must have drank five quarts of crap rum that night, and a gallon of pure grain alcohol, chased it with an eighteen-inch thin crust with pepperoni and bacon. NO FUCKING OLIVES. One time I broke my arm. Who cares, it's all gone, but that smell, the horrid taste of gastric juices and garlic remains.

Decades later, I'm buying greasy slices at a Sbarro, trying to fold and eat them, dripping hot grease all over my Mariah Carey tour shirt. A guy in front of the Wendy's on Broadway handed me a Makita power drill. It was one of the rechargeable ones, with the huge battery coming out of the handle, and a drill bit you'd use to bore through the reinforced concrete walls of a bank vault or prison cell. It felt heavy and expensive, maybe with diamonds in the bit. They aren't like Kay jeweler diamonds in there, but they still aren't cheap.

"Carry on my wayward son." The man had the hair and beard of someone from a lost desert island with no civilization or Supercuts. The drill was covered in powder, like plaster or concrete powder. I mean, it could have been flour — I don't know if Wendy's bakes their own bread in-house, or they ship it in from the suburbs or Atlanta or Vietnam. I didn't lick it to see what it tasted like.

"I don't want a fucking drill. I want one of those quarter-pound bacon cheese burgers. I don't care what Jon Stewart bullshit propaganda you flyover assholes believe, but a slice isn't a meal. Ten slices isn't a meal. Soup isn't a meal, either. What the hell am I supposed to do with a drill?" Also, they weren't quarter pounders — that's the other guys, legally registered trademark and all. They tried calling them one-third pound burgers, but nobody knows that a third of a pound is bigger than a quarter-pound, and it failed. Bring back the old lady, she can sell burgers. Or the hot redhead. Don't bring math into this. America wants calories, not fractions.

"No, you want drill. Drill for happy!" He pushed the power tool into my hands, getting dust all over my greasy Mariah Carey shirt, forming a slurry that would later harden like cement. I slapped him across the face like an old-timey black-and-white film star slaps his bitch up, screaming "DON"T FUCK WITH MY SHIRT! MARIAH CAREY IS PUNK AS FUCK!" He dropped to the sidewalk and the chicken nuggets (not Chicken McNuggets, trademark again) fell out of his pockets onto the sidewalk. A gaggle of school kids in uniforms rushed over from a nearby bus stop and grabbed the chunks of cold chicken from the concrete, and ate them with no sauce — fucking savages.

I thought about what the man said as I ducked into an insurance agency next to the Wendy's. (It may have been a map store or a luggage store — it was downstairs from a Jiu Jitsu place that was also a driving academy.) I think he was talking in a code, something with song lyrics and famous last words from totalitarian leaders. One of the former Soviet satellite states had a leader — or maybe the leader's wife — who said "drill for happy" right before being shot on live TV. I can't remember *who*. I didn't have a firm grasp on the geopolitical situation back in 1989, 1990 — I was trying to get laid, unsuccessfully coping with the terrain of my freshman year of college.

This was back before Wikipedia, google — any of the web, really. My facts and urban legends were intermingled, and I remember telling a first date that the Japanese language had no verbs — something I think I heard on a Yngwie Malmsteen album — and then when she doubted me, I had to keep doubling down, hoping she wouldn't drag me to a library at two in the morning to search through microfiche until she proved I was an idiot. I guess she could have asked a Japanese major or a Japanese-speaking foreign exchange student, but we were all freshman and Undecided majors, and the Japanese speaker wouldn't be able to articulate this with a lack of verbs, right?

The one upside to trying to get to second base with this genius was we ended up listening to the first Mariah Carey album a dozen times. I think it stuck with me because of the typical reasons, the slowed-down ballads and novelty of her voice. But then I read up on the pedigree of studio musicians used on the album, a crew of the top talent that was in New York at the end of the 80s. Like the guitar duties were split between Living Colour's Vernon Reid, Booker T. Jones music director Vernon "Ice" Black, and a half-dozen other names who had played on albums from Michael Jackson to INXS to Daft Punk to Lady Gaga. Marcus Miller, fresh off a decade of albums with Miles Davis, played bass. The piano was covered by Richard Tee, who played half of Peter Gabriel's So album a few years prior. Walter Afanasieff, later an integral producing talent for Carey, covered horns and synth; this was ten years before he would win a Grammy for producing Celine Dion's "My Heart Will Go On." Basically Mariah Carey is like the Kevin Bacon of studio musicians of the 80s and 90s. Mariah Carey is punk as fuck.

I walked back to the queer book store where I originally bought my t-shirt, the one with magic manuals and amulets of toenails and incense, designed to bring you health and wealth. (These are not medical claims evaluated by the FDA, for entertainment value only.) I was hoping they could get me a replacement for under $40, even though honestly, I should just cut the shit with wearing t-shirts of bands and go to solid colors, because it's not like wearing a band t-shirt makes you a better person or unique in any way, like I thought it did for the last few decades. The guy at the counter dressed in crystals told a guy on the phone he formed a splinter faction of Alcoholics Anonymous that had 786 steps, and by step 700, they gave you your own planet in the afterlife, and every person you killed would be your slave after you died. Still no last names, just letters. He said he was Johnny X. I didn't believe him.

They didn't have the shirt. I don't care. (They did have that crust punk/bass fishing zine, but I already had the newest issue, and the next one wouldn't be released for ten more years.) I could not trust the shop owner with my personal details to order a replacement. I don't trust anyone on this planet except G.G. Allin and that hot redheaded chick from the Wendy's commercials. They both deal with human shit, and that's the only kind of person you can trust anymore.

* * *

"I don't know..." Back in the McDonald's the wormy dude ogled the Game Boy, looking for any excuse to low-ball me or back out of the deal. "It looks okay, but it's the generic yellow version, and I was sort of holding out for the Hello Kitty Special Box 2 Japanese limited-edition with the light pink case. It would be nice if it had the original box and manual, too. This isn't just any old time portal we're trading for."

I grabbed the Game Boy out of his greasy hands, ran for the door, and later threw the portable game console in the garbage in front of a Duane Reade. I didn't need this shit. I didn't need a time portal. I didn't need anything. I don't know what I need anymore.

The Third-Generation Camaro Is Not Cult and Satanic Enough for Our Slut-Fucking Requirements, Duane

"Left hand path, the devil's mark." Duane the Satanic Arby's cashier ignored the endless line of drive-through customers and helped me arrange a bag of frozen french fries into the shape of a pentagram. He hummed some Slayer from the *God Hates Us All* album, while I snorted horsey sauce from a tube next to the cash register, for effect. "We will summon Satan," Duane chanted, "use his majestic powers to conjure a new car so we can fuck sluts. I'm thinking a Z-28, either red or black. All hail Arby's!"

Me and Duane go way back, since a computer camp our respective parents forced us to attend in the summer between sixth and seventh grade. I wrote a *Barney Miller* video game for the Commodore Plus Four computer, and he sketched out some Abe Vigoda 8-bit images on graph paper for me. He lost all artistic ability and fully embraced Satanism after he got a traumatic brain injury; he fell off a ladder trying to sky-jerk to a video of a slutty shoe cobbler with open heart surgery scars. He's still a cool dude, despite his frequent seizures. He also gives me free curly fries.

"I've got a brother-in-law-slash-cousin selling a fuckin' 1989 IROC-Z with the hidden IROC level 0 option," he said, wielding a grill spatula like a young Jean-Claude swinging a sword. "In that year, if you deleted the air conditioning, they put on an aluminum drive shaft, bigger rotors, stiffer suspension, all that SCCA racing shit. It's like a secret menu item so they could include all the hi-po cop options on a stock model. He also sawed holes in the doors to put in giant fucking speakers so he could listen to power metal at proper volume. The seats smell like piss, though. His old lady's a squirter."

I vomited a mixture of blood and horseradish, projectile-puking all the way across the back line trays of condiments and ingredients. For a split-second, while the root vegetable sauce burned through my head cavities and into my brain, I saw a vision of a sweaty, naked Dennis Hopper teaching a mommy Zumba class in a church basement in Toledo, Ohio. He lactated profusely as a Pitbull song blared from the sound system, and said something profound that I didn't entirely understand, like "free love," or "free yourself," or "free your mind." Maybe he was in hell and said "free me," I don't know. A quick snort of Jamocha shake righted my sinuses, and stopped the explosion of pain hallucinations. "How much does he want for the Z-28? If it's cheap enough, you could mod that shit up, put in a crate motor and a smoke machine, for dark magic purposes."

"It's an IROC-Z, not a Z-28. They didn't have a Z-28 that year because everyone was busy jerking off to Milli Vanilli or Richard Marks or whatever. He's asking six thousand six hundred and sixty six dollars, and sixty-six cents, not a penny less. He needs to pay restitution on these four kids he crippled when he ran over them on a DUI chase last year. It didn't fuck up the car though. Kids have soft bones, and it's got urethane bumpers and spoilers."

"I wouldn't pay four hundred tops for that car, including the stereo and a full tank of premium gas. I'd tear out the drivetrain, sell the electronics, and dump the rest in a river. Those Knight Rider-looking pieces of shit are not cult and satanic enough. I'm thinking you need to buy an old hearse, go straight *Harold and Maude*, but like with some side pipes, a chrome blower sticking out of the hood, and a really obnoxious stereo. Bluetooth, too."

A guy who looked like the lesbian Paul McCartney came into the restaurant, sprinkling holy water on everything around him. His aspergillum was custom-built at a Czech Republic liturgical supply house with *Harry Potter* inscriptions and sigils on it. A blast of the water hit Duane behind the counter, and he fell to the floor, screaming the "it burns!" line from *The Exorcist*.

"Hey man, watch where you swing that thing, champ," I said. "Some of us are susceptible to the alleged powers of sacramental materials. Order your roast beef and get the fuck out."

"I'm not here to eat roast beef. I saw the 'HAIL SATAN' sign on the front of the store and wanted to tell a cautionary tale about how I was playing the board game Carrom, but I was using an Ouija board, and summoned the ghost of dead Richard Lewis from hell."

"Richard Lewis isn't dead. I just saw him on that show with the bald *Star Trek* dude, Captain Piccard."

"He did invent the '...from hell' line though," lesbian Paul McCartney said. "And I didn't say this was a true story. I just said it was *a* story. It's a cautionary tale, and I'm trying to help you out, you cocksucker."

"That's a bullshit move," Duane said. He'd soaked his face and hands with a spray bottle of buffalo dipping sauce to rinse away the holy water, then started chewing on a piece of raw brisket that had fallen on the floor. "Any time you tell a story that you're in, you're implying it's true."

"What about gonzo journalism, though?" I said. "I mean, if I tell a story, like that I'm hanging out with my friend Duane in an Arby's, and it's all in the first person, I'm implying it's true, but really I'm using it as a set piece to make up a story. Like when Hunter Thompson wrote the Vegas book, he wasn't necessarily saying he did everything he described; he was telling a story and creating the reality around it."

"Yeah, but he *was* in Vegas. Maybe he fudged the details, but that was mostly a true story."

"SO RICHARD LEWIS IS IN HELL. THIS IS MY STORY, BRO. RICHARD LEWIS IS IN HELL."

"Wait, was *Curb Your Enthusiasm* a documentary, or all scripted? Like, is that really Larry David's life, or are they making all that up?" Duane went off on these meta tirades, which usually signaled he was about to have a seizure, and I started looking around for something to shove in his mouth so he wouldn't swallow his tongue. "Because Richard Lewis was in *Curb*, and was that a persona, or based on events in his life, or was it really truth and they put it in the show? Like did he really need a kidney transplant? Was Jeff Garland really his manager?"

There was a rack of free newspapers next to the door, and I picked one up, to see if I could fold it in half and jam it between his teeth before the seizure hit, but then I opened it up and started reading an article that caught my interest. It was about some crazy bitch who blazed across Kansas in a busted-up minivan with her three kids strapped in the back, each one shot ten times and decapitated. She ran out of gas somewhere on I-70 and hitchhiked to a truck stop with a horny long-haul driver who sold her into white slavery. The cops found the van days later, the FM stereo blasting "Can't

Fight This Feeling." Years later, someone would file for Social Security in her name, and even receive benefits for a while, but the government found it was was just an imposter, and they would never find the real mother.

The killings, the thought of the killings haunted me, in the same way I became fixated on the world's tallest man, some freak from Peoria who never stopped producing growth hormone and became nine feet tall before he mutilated his leg trying to fuck a threshing machine and died of gangrene after a month of begging for someone to kill him. I remember he tried eating a pound of pure opium to end his suffering, but he weighed so much, it didn't even give him a buzz. And his dick was two feet long soft, as big around as an oil can. They even had a fold-out life-sized picture of it in the *Guinness Book*. Wore regular length jeans that looked like jorts, his dong hanging out of the bottom of the leg. (He dressed left.)

And I knew a girl who reminded me of the patricide mom, a dumpy religious nut who always wore gingham dresses, and looked like she could be a sister wife in some remote Utah compound filled with paranoid assholes stockpiling ammo and spam, waiting for the end of the world. (Why do you stockpile stuff if you're going to rapture, anyway? Seems like you'd just install a good breakaway sunroof and leave it at that.) I think her name was Judy or Jen or something predictable like that. We both worked dead-end office jobs, different departments, but swapped emails all day, about the mundane, real work-spouse kind of shit. I thought if I could get her to forget about the Jesus for a few minutes, I could at least swap a dinner at the mall for a reluctant hand job in my car. But she eventually moved to some lockdown bible college in Stockton or Vallejo or one of those dead-end California towns that went bankrupt and traded all their cop cars for meth.

"The dream is dead," said the editorial page. "We can no longer be held accountable for the honor killings in the name of organic vegetables. Meat for murder! Fuck all legumes! Soon they'll be here with flamethrowers!" I think the free newspaper guy was in the middle of a stroke as he dictated his latest column to a minimum-wage typist who didn't even proof the thing before running it. Ernie Pyle would take a shit down the throat of 97% of the news industry now. Race to the bottom — content is king, but let's not fool ourselves, we won't pay for it.

"WHAT THE FUCK IS CURB? WHAT THE FUCK IS CURB?" Duane's mouth was foaming, and I knew he was moments from a grand mal. "And why do you set so many of your stories in Arby's? You've seriously had at least one per book, if not more. Did you used to work at Arby's?"

"No. I did work next to an Arby's for a summer, slinging tacos at a drive-through. And I guess I've fucked out a disproportionate number of Arby's managers for some reason, back in the day. I don't know if that says something about my taste in women, or Arby's hiring standards. I always preferred Rax Roast Beef, but I think they went bankrupt. The one I used to go to got converted into a Chinese buffet that sells bootleg golf clubs at the salad bar..."

"LET ME TELL MY STORY. THIS IS TRUE. RICHARD LEWIS IS IN HELL. THE BOARD WILL SUMMON HIM. THIS IS A CAUTIONARY TALE, YOU PIECE OF SHIT. DO NOT GO DOWN THE DARK PATH."

"Shut the fuck up, lesbian Paul McCartney. Go trade your fuckin' holy water sprinkler for a back-alley facelift. You look like fucking Leatherface from the *Texas Chainsaw Massacre* with all that loose skin hanging off your skull." Duane pulled out his double-barrel sawed off shotgun, loaded with Bronco Berry sauce instead of buckshot, and blasted a load into the ceiling. Everyone hit the ground or ran, save one old deaf guy who had been nursing the same senior citizen coffee for the last six hours.

I went back to my french fries, picking at the smaller crusty ones while waiting for Duane to go comatose from his seizure. But the fries were stone cold, and there's no reheating those fucking things. This story may or may not be true, but that is.

The Whole Country Is Built on an Indian Burial Ground and We Are All Going To Die So Stop Trying to Fuck with Me About How a Sonic Shake Has Two Thousand Calories

We drove to a Sonic hamburger stand after the cult's story broke, the endless social media hand-wringing creating an insufferable hunger that overpriced potato chips from the vending machine on the third floor would not satisfy. Bury 14 people in a school bus in the middle of the desert with nothing but jars of urine and a single bag of fun-size Kit-Kat bars, and you'll shoot straight to the top of the headline news tragedy exploitation rotation faster than a reality star's fat greased ass hanging out of the back of her expensive dress. You'll only stay there a day though, until someone's kid takes a dump on the conveyor belt at a Safeway cash register and the video goes viral. Warhol promised everyone fifteen minutes, but it's now more like three page reloads, tops.

I knew the main cult dude, Melvil, a freaky, castrated comic book guy who somehow convinced people to join his Away Team and make the big transition to the comet in the sky. Fat Mike knew him too — we all went to high school together, and got the shit beat of us on a daily basis by the fundamentalist football-o-fascists. Melvil got into pills, hardcore ADHD stuff at first. His dad drove a forklift at a pharmaceutical manufacturing company, so he had the hookup on the good shit. He would get huge jugs of thousands of Desoxyn tablets for a dollar at the employee store. Things unspooled from there.

Fat Mike and I sat in the Sonic, sucking down high-calorie milkshakes with impunity. Mikey lamented over the cultists, and reports of their pharmaceutical habits. "My uncle got killed by a bunch of pill-heads when I was a kid," he said. "Damnedest thing. They were tripped out on a mix of toad venom and Obertol."

"I've never heard of Obertol. It sounds like an old cholesterol medicine."

"It's speed they sold to dumpy housewives trying to lose weight back in the Fifties. The mix of the two caught on because of Walter Cronkie's pool boy, who did mighty amounts of the combo and then tried to jump off the Golden Gate Bridge dressed as the Hamburglar. It was in an old issue of *Grit* magazine."

"Yeah, I think I saw a made-for-TV movie about it, with George Clooney."

"That's the one. This cult went door-to-door in a old army surplus truck painted day-glo orange, handing out ditto sheets of their shitty manifesto. They told everyone they had pieces of the frozen head of Martin Bormann for sale. Said the iced brain chunks would give the owner mystical healing powers and enable them to time travel. Poor old Uncle Freddy called bullshit on this, and one of the drifters killed him by sinking the cuticle file on a pair of Coty toenail clippers into his jugular vein."

The Sonic gave free unlimited refills on our frozen drinks, but we had to endure their wait staff to get them. The kids working there were the imperfect combination of nerdy and idiotic, like teenagers who just smoked weed for the first time last week and had to spend an hour telling you about Bob Marley and that time Ford built a car out of hemp. We ate salty tater tots and convulsed from brain freeze while a roller-skated geek preached on about illegal ColecoVision mod kits from Uganda. "I'm ordering a copy of the Expansion Module #1 that emulates the NORAD launch system. I'm gonna start a nuclear war against the Soviet Union. I just need a better power conditioning setup so I don't keep burning out the graphics chips."

"Keep babbling about germanium diodes like you know what you're talking about, you dumbass," I mumbled. "The world's falling apart, and you're jerking off to a 1976 Radio Shack catalog. Good luck with that after they close the last location and turn it into a Mexican dollar store." He did not listen to me, and another round of brain freeze hit, sending me images of Xavier Nady's second career as a freelance unlicensed plumber in Sedona, wiring in sink fixtures upside down and backwards, the ill-fitting copper u-joints rotting a vivid green, like the Statue of Liberty at Woodstock, dosing the brown acid while Jimi wailed away in a 79-minute guitar solo during "Free Bird."

"You're supposed to touch your tongue to the roof of your mouth when you get brain freeze," Fat Mike yelled at me. "Stupid fuck! Tongue! Roof of mouth! God damn it, you do this every time you drink anything colder than pond water!" I shut off the radio and beat my head against the dash until "SRS AIRBAG" was indented in my brow in reverse like a burn scar from a fraternity branding iron.

We threw out the soggy food and split, peeling out of the parking lot and driving down the wrong side of the road at high speed. I'd recently picked up a habit for prednisone, something I scored off of a buddy who had a double kidney transplant and didn't keep up with the anti-rejection meds out of some insane Jesus-based rationale about luck and fate. The steroids gave me an inhuman amount of road rage, and driving became a tortuous experience where I'd scream at inanimate objects like light posts and landscaping water features, thinking they were about to kill me. I could quit at any time, though.

"I haven't seen Toad for months." Fat Mike went off on some conversational tangent as I fought for control of the car, and I didn't completely follow his story. "He got caught jerking off on stage at a Pearl Jam concert in Iowa. Eddie Vedder was cool with it, I guess, but it was at an Indian casino and he got hauled in for a hate crime."

"Wait, who is Toad? Is he the guy who flew a 747 into a Wal-Mart to get an erection?"

"No, this is the zine guy, the one we used to call Toad Pickledick, who used to work on *Law and Order*. He sent me a jar of Vlasik pickles with a severed cock in them. Anyway, dude had some oxy in his car, his grandma's prescription. He had to sell all his CDs online to pay his legal bills. I got a copy of that first Pungent Stench album for five bucks, and a couple of those gold-plated Zappa CDs. I don't know if they sound any better, though. I mean, maybe they did some remaster filtered stuff, PCM or PZM or PCP or whatever the hell they call it, but that's not magic, it's just a fucking album about eating poo."

"I think it was Alice Cooper that ate poo, not Frank Zappa. Or maybe he played golf. I don't need a history of CD remastering, I just want to know if he still published that zine *Mandatory Laxative*. I read the issue where he wrote all those letters to former Secretary of Commerce Philip Klutznick, asking him about Jimmy Carter's UFO sightings. I don't think he knew Klutznick died in 1999, or maybe that was part of the joke."

"Yeah he doesn't do that zine any more. Zines are stupid. Fuck the post office, just make a tumblr blog of dick pics and look at tits online. Nobody's ever going to pay to read something someone wrote."

We drove south, through the nothingness, hoping to see a glimpse of Melvil's cult ranch. I played with the headlights, flipping the controls on and off. Something about the tactile click of the knob on the end of the turn signal stalk made it oddly satisfying to cycle through the settings: FOG, HL, PARK, OFF, DRL, then DRL, OFF, PARK, HL, FOG. Then back to HL — it wasn't foggy out, didn't want to burn out the battery prematurely in case we got stranded in the woods, surviving on forest fires started with the juice from a dome light.

"You ever get your hair cut at a JC Penney's salon? I think they filter their water with mind-control vitamins and minerals. I went there once as a kid, and I had nightmares for a month, terror dreams about buying spaghetti in Astoria, Queens, taking it on the C train to the World Trade

Center, while that Boston song about feelings played on repeat. And then Al Roker came on the train, ate all my spaghetti, but he'd already had that stomach-staple surgery at that point, so my gallon of bulk pasta made him explode like that fat dude in the movie *Seven*. And the weird part is I'd never been to New York at that point in my childhood. And the C train doesn't even run to Astoria. That's an IND train, and it's all BMT out in Queens. The closest BMT is the Cortlandt Street N/R, a block east."

"I don't think the minerals from a cut and rinse would do that much damage," I said. "Even if it was straight-up Love Canal water in that hair sink, you wouldn't absorb that much. You probably had a traumatic head injury as a kid."

"At least it wasn't traumatic ball injury. That's where Melvil got the whole castration thing. One time, we were riding BMX bikes around the hood, and he was trying to jump a ditch out behind Spiro Agnew middle school, and totally didn't stick the landing. Went balls-first into the handlebar stem, and everyone in a five-block radius who had a pair dropped to the ground moaning. He limped home and pissed blood in the sink for like ten minutes straight."

"Jesus christ, it hurts just hearing that story."

"At least we won't have to worry about any Melvil juniors if he ever managed to get lucky and fuck one of his cult members without a rubber."

We drove to the random field behind a Target super-store, following miles of dirt roads unmapped on my vintage 2007 GPS, looking for the compound where Melvil ran his empire. In the distance, we saw a state prison's klieg lights on sniper towers, large stainless steel signs saying "We kill sexual deviants and solicitors." A chain gang of serial rapists and mass-murders sat on folding chairs, selling garbage bags filled with baked goods made out of reshaped chunks of confinement loaf.

"We have to stop," Fat Mike said. "Imagine if you had the chance to buy a bundt cake from Charlie Manson and you passed it up because you were in a hurry to get back to work and do your weekly status report."

"Work? Fuck that shit. Pabst Blue Ribbon!" I e-braked to a stop on the side of the road and struck up a conversation with a toothless federal wiretapping inmate chained to a guy doing a lifetime sentence for unpaid parking tickets. He handed me a sheet of stale, deformed pastries, coated in a thick layer of chocolate frosting. The pan of muffins looked like the Marianas Trench, a screaming mess of raw chicken and the blood of a thousand dead coal miners, stirred into ten boxes of reddi-mix corn cake batter. Each of the eight cylinders of doom contained sprinkles made from stem cell research and Satanic offerings to our dark lord, and the muffin mongoloids twisted and screamed with life and death, each a biochemical experiment in horror. "The world is a series of tubes," the inmate told me. "Series of tubes. Trust nobody."

Fat Mike always carried a battery-powered moto-tool with diamond cutting blades. He got off on sawing things in half: appliances at department stores, cars in parking lots, dinosaur bones at the natural history museum. One time I watched him carefully dissect every piece of an oil drilling rig in East Texas, from crown block to drill bit. He pulled out his grinder, and fastened a new cutting wheel, while carefully eyeing the guard in mirrorshades slinging a *Cool Hand Luke* style shotgun.

"Cover me. We've got to take this dude with us. He knows how to hack payroll computers. We could change our timecards and never show up again. Goldbrick level: expert." He started fake-coughing like a chain-smoker with tuberculosis to cover the sound of the Dremel EZ Lock wheel. I stood in front of the duo and talked loudly to everybody and nobody, explaining my paranoid theories about how the aluminum in baking powder is going to cause Alzheimer's in a generation of bread fans, that gluten isn't the issue. Fat Mike broke the guy's shackles in no time flat, and we crawled into my tiny Toyota Yaris, driving at five below the speed limit to avoid suspicion.

"That cult guy wasn't out here," said the inmate. "He bought a vacant lot in the desert, next to the prison. Used to go to conjugal visits at the pen, with this dumpy bus driver-looking chick with a four-foot-wide ass. Tax evasion, I think.

I don't know why he got the visits if he didn't have a pair. But he said he couldn't run the cult from out here in unincorporated Marshall county because of building codes. You can't live in a school bus for more than 14 days without an extended camping permit, and the county won't ever issue one."

"Fucking fascists," Fat Mike said. "Can't the government let a no-ball dude talk about UFOs in peace?"

Fields of tulips dotted with Syrian land mines drew the tourists to a fake amusement park next to the not-a-mall outdoor mall. Old people with fanny packs and ancient cameras stepped on live ordinance while snapping pictures of the spring bloom of the flowers. A massage parlor on the edge of the theme park catered to amputees, offering full-stump deep tissue work, 10% off for veterans or seniors with an AARP membership. They also sold astronaut ice cream and chunks of broken cinderblocks and cut up car sheet metal they said were pieces of the Berlin Wall and World Trade Center — any gambit to get the tourists to empty their wallets, $40 t-shirts that disintegrated after three washings, and ten-dollar hot dogs bought in bulk at Sam's Club for a nickel each.

"This was all built on an ancient Indian burial ground," the inmate said. "They tried to grow one of those mazes so we could kill Jack Nicholson during the winter season — not the real dude, but like a kid that can do a Jack impression for minimum wage. Double irony because they were growing a maze out of corn — a maize maze. But there's something wrong with the soil structure. Can't grow weed, either. Fucking Indians."

"The whole country is built on an Indian burial ground," I told him. "We are all going to die. You, me, the person reading this: you will all die. Keep drinking kombucha and doing cross-fit. You WILL die. Everyone dies. Even god died. That German fuck wrote about it, Nostradamus or whatever."

The mountain altitude and prednisone tablets made me ravenous 24/7, and caused a sinus drainage that smelled like broken technology and doom. I wanted to find a book store to look up more about this Indian burial ground/plant growing disorder thing, preferably one with a cafe that sold hot sandwiches. Maybe the Indians added ground up bones in the topsoil? Wasn't this in *Guns, Germs, and Steel?* I was sure I could find a dozen idiots from here to the end of the street selling fake arrowheads who would tell me whatever I wanted to hear, for a small fee. But nothing is truth when everything is available.

We parked behind a spur line of the old railroad and scraped the black soot off the side of a Union Pacific Diesel engine, collecting the oxidized paint and pollution flakes, and cut it into a fine, snortable powder, for later use on an all-night bender of sodomy and arson. Decades before, enterprising youth would derail trains just to masturbate to the images of a hundred-car freighter plunging into a gulch. A very freudian orgasm, old-school angst and despair, the kind of thing that would make a proper coke fiend proud. Now it's all about streaming porn, electric train games on the iPhone. You can't even find good pictures of a tasty bridge explosion. Times have changed.

Sleep Letter Zero

An old man gets on the BMT train during rush hour, limping. He pushes an aluminum walker covered in old punk stickers and dog shit. He looks about 150 years old, but he's really 68. He has shingles.

He hands everyone a pamphlet about orthopedic mattresses. The pamphlets were printed in Chinatown, and smell like paint thinner.

"I want you all to imagine your Sleep Letter." He yells over the bing-bong sound of the doors closing. "Imagine your Sleep Letter!"

A kitchen knife salesman squeezes through the closing doors. He looks like a fetish guy who enjoys getting gang-raped on a pool table. His nicotine-colored shirt doesn't match his wide silk tie. The tie consists of more food stains than original colors. His hair is severely parted to one side, like an autistic software developer from the Eighties.

The knife salesman looks at a woman with the ass of Beyoncé and the face of Tracy Morgan. "I haven't jerked off since the Space Shuttle exploded," he mumbles. He doesn't specify which Space Shuttle. He bumps into the walker.

"Your Sleep Letter is zero, sir!" The old man doesn't explain the Sleep Letter thing, or why the letter is a number.

Everyone imagines 100 is the best, and their bed ranges between a 70 and mid-40s.

A girl with a neckbeard across the train car from the knife man starts licking her pamphlet. She moans, like a trucker taking a dump after a long haul with no rest areas. She has a single, thick eyebrow, which makes her look angry all the time. She's actually pretty chill; she takes a high dose of Ativan.

The Dominican kid next to her studies a black and white photocopied magazine of conjoined twin porn, while rubbing his crotch. His jeans are sized to fit a large statue of Paul Bunyan in front of a hardware store. They fall down when he walks, and rub together like a person trying to start a fire in the wilderness.

The zine is titled *Maxxximum ChangnEng*. It has a foldout of Chang and Eng Bunker in an orgy with four workers from the P.T. Barnum circus. They released five issues before the publisher got his girlfriend pregnant and dropped out of the zine scene to work as a janitor for an elementary school in Arizona.

The Dominican ignores everyone, and licks his lips. He's holding the zine close to his face, and needs to see an eye doctor. His eyes require +7 diopters of correction for farsightedness. His daily use of cannabis has cured a mild case of glaucoma.

The old man sings the theme to *Happy Days*, but changes the word "happy" to "crappy." A subway cop from Yonkers runs into the car and starts beating him with his own walker.

When the train stops at Queensborough Plaza, the knife guy pretends he only speaks Dutch ("Bij ons noemt men dit een dorp") and runs from the police. He's dismembered 27 people, and the remains are in his third floor apartment. He's eaten four of the bodies, and is making a human throne from pieces of a ribcage. The police catch him a year later, after he uses a dead person's Metro card. He pleads insanity and gets a book deal. His book sells two orders of magnitude more than anything I've ever published.

The old man dies of an aneurysm before the N train reaches Ditmars. The police claim he was armed, and tell the press about his 1947 misdemeanor fraud charge.

(There's a bootleg Dunkin' Donuts at Queensborough Plaza, but don't waste your time.)

The Metaphor of Poundcake

"We seek comfort in patterns." I awoke to a cop talking truth and fantasy while taking a piss on the cardboard cutout of Barbara Bush in my fireplace. "Each of us look to the future in determination, to help us feel at peace with the present. But we will never reach it."

The police officer moaned and started to piss blood, a brown, chunky, sewerage stream of bacteria-infested kidney disease and failure. "Celebrate the journey of the natural hierarchy, the sacred path of the warrior." He shook twice, zipped up, then grabbed his nightstick from his belt holster and smashed my commemorative Alan Alda urn, containing the ashes of my great-uncle Theodore, a habitual peyote user and manager of a mini-mart on an Indian reservation in Oklahoma. "Never stray from the path. And clean your kitchen. It looks like an anthrax research lab in there."

* * *

I must have fallen asleep waiting for the phone call about Virgil's execution. The fever dream of the evening involved walking on a desolate college campus in the waning, vanishing hours of what I thought was the immaculate romance, something that happened for a third of my life, causing me to wonder if the dream really did happen.

It took sixteen hours of travel to get to the campus from the city: three trains, two layovers, and a four-mile walk in a snowstorm that caused my wheeled suitcase to flail around like a subcompact car with bald tires on an ice skating rink. I lost a dozen pounds during the journey, like a baseball pitcher putting in the nine full innings of a complete game, all of the labor from fidgeting in my seat and trying not to throttle the man sitting across from me, who kept babbling about alternate realities and stock speculation. The train had no food, the bar car destroyed by a group of abolitionist terrorists who didn't understand the basic fact that you could drink an entire 401K's worth of alcohol on an Amtrak and not get drunk. This was a government venture; of course they water down the drinks to the point of absurdity. Uncle Sam's not going to get you fucked up on top-shelf liquor.

In the weeks of phone calls and emails prior to the voyage, I was promised unlimited sex, all-you-can eat of her young ass, and as many trips to Denny's as I could muster. But we both managed to catch a destructive viral pneumonia that no amount of over-the-counter syrups or pills could touch. The closest we got to the promised week of torrid, unprotected sex was a midnight brunch at a place that served almost raw eggs Benedict and a reluctant handjob in the parking lot. (Come to think of it, those eggs could have been how we got sick.)

After a two-day puke and shit marathon, I spent the rest of the week killing time in a motel while she went to work.

My only solace in the high fever hallucination state was a hack I found in 2600 magazine article on cable phreaking. A magic code enabled me to watch all of the Nineties-era soft-core porn for free, an endless stream of basketball-sized tit implants, frizzy hair, long *Predator*-like whore nails, and over-enthusiastic fake lesbian threesomes. How did they finger so much with inch-long long acrylic press-on nails? And why did my breath smell like a Seventies landfill? This sickness was killing me, even in my dream, like those Freddy Kreuger movies.

Desperate for a lunch other than the year-old extruded peanut butter and cheese crackers from the motel lobby vending machine, I stumbled outside, and tried to hoof it to a Wendy's Hamburgers distant on the horizon. Its sign, with the cartoon ponytailed redhead, stood atop a five hundred foot steel pole, telling people on the highway to pull over and meet their maker, for only $2.99 plus tax. I crossed a series of grassy knoll medians, which chopped apart a grocery store parking lot from a series of used car dealerships, forming a maze of torment that threatened to face-plant me into the asphalt with every dozen steps.

A man painted on the windshield of an old Chevy with white shoe polish, spelling out "ELECTRONIC CAR" and a price point that seemed too good to be true. The front of the car rose from the ground at a sharp angle, like a converted low-rider with air shocks, about to launch from the ground in a sideshow parking-lot maneuver. I could tell, even at a distance, that some asshole tore out the old V-8 and hastily Rube Goldberged some kind of household appliance motor into the front, maybe a powered golf cart's drivetrain.

"It's a real electronic," the used car salesman told me. His jacket looked like the tablecloth to a defunct pizza joint from the Seventies, and he reeked of cheap cigar smoke. "You can apply for the tax credit and everything. I don't have the paperwork here, but I'm sure the DMV can set you up. You don't do much highway driving, do you son? It only tops out at about 38 kilometers an hour. But it gets a thousand miles a gallon, theoretical. And lots of torque. Torque is all you need. Torque wins you races. Torque is Jesus. Torque from Ork — nanu nanu! How's your credit, boy?"

I kept walking past, turned up the headphones and blasted the Anal Cunt tape louder, so I would not exist, be invisible. I needed food, fried food, heavy, grease-laden food to survive. Lay down a bed of solid grease, and you can ride out any chronic diarrhea. My temperature was at least 104, and everything looked like a direct-to-video John Carpenter movie about Armenia. I wanted a frozen beverage and enough extra bacon to kill god. I wanted this dream to end, but after I woke, I sort of wished it would continue.

* * *

I muted the TV, found a spiral notebook and a pen. The ballpoint was from an Uncle Kenny's Sex Dungeon in

Wailea, the one in the basement of the Maui Four Seasons. The plastic barrel was covered in tooth marks, which I hoped were only mine. I thought about death a lot that week, with Virgil on the way out. I hastily prepared a note:

> In the event of my death, I want a funeral where my body is not embalmed or preserved. It will be propped upside down on a geodesic dome playground monkey bar thing, like the cover of the first Suicidal Tendencies album. There will be no Pepsi. Donate my orthotic inserts to the Salvador Dali motorcycle museum in Clearwater, Florida (NOT the Salvador Dali museum in St. Petersburg. They are false prophets.) Serve Taco Bell Doritos Locos tacos at the reception. DO NOT invite my cousin Marty or his whore wife, because not only will they will eat all of the fucking tacos, they will only eat the meat and cheese and lick the shells but not eat them, and then they won't shut the fuck up about how carbs are an evil conspiracy to keep us all fat. Play "Free Bird" on repeat, and the first person to suggest that it should be turned off should be buried alive in the coffin and grave I purchased ten plots down from Bruce and Brandon Lee's crypt at Lake View cemetery in Seattle. Burn my body and have everyone snort the ashes. Don't forget the thing about Marty. I finger-fucked his wife at Thanksgiving dinner in 1987. I'm not proud of this, but it was before they

were married, and I'm dead now, so fuck it. Peace out.

I read the note carefully, chugging from a warm can of Meister-Brau, then sealed it in an envelope and put it on the fireplace mantle, now an altar to broken urns and diseased cop blood. Having a friend get killed makes you question your own mortality, and that was about to happen.

* * *

Virgil had a dad that got the electric chair for mortgage fraud when we were ten, an absurd irony in the wake of his own pending death sentence. Virg Senior was the kind of old-school, trapped-in-the-past dad that still slicked his hair back with Brylcreem like a Sha Na Na reject. He talked about chopped deuces and daddy-o's while we cringed and hoped nobody at the mall saw us with him. After his old man rode the lightning, Virgil went from bad to worse, a series of alcoholic and drug-addled stepfathers that beat him like a used golf ball at a driving range. He finally decided to run away, leave the state with ten dollars in change and a stolen LaserDisc player he'd fence for weed money somewhere in rural Nebraska.

I got the post card months later: no return address, no name signed, just a picture of the country's third-largest ear of corn, on the outskirts of some town in Iowa or Montana or Laos, a car-sized husk with two goofy farmers in front of it. The inscription said "FOUND YOU'RE MOM'S DIL-DO!" in sharpie, with a smaller note scrawled in ballpoint, his unmistakable, illegible cursive. "Met a shower curtain salesman — let's dudes bang his wife in motels — said he'd give me his car if I sucked his dick — just borrowing it for now — his wife's a good lay, but too quiet — will send pics — fuck the puke, and Jesus! — V" I hoped he meant fuck the puke and fuck Jesus. I didn't want a 3 AM phone call of drunken bible platitudes from a borderline illiterate high school dropout. I already got that pretty much every day when I went to public school in Indiana.

I brought the card to my state-appointed therapist. During the breaking-the-ice meeting, she told me she saw *Forrest Gump* 200 times and only wanted to date mentally disabled men. I think it was supposed to turn me on. I've slept with enough mental health care professionals to know the warning signs, but also knew you always hold out for someone who can prescribe drugs. Even if you don't want the drugs, even if you're one of those health food freaks who isn't into the idea of loading up on deadly narcotics, you get the doc who can write for meds, because then you know they love you. Love is drugs. I saw it on a t-shirt once; it must be true.

After therapy, I paced the halls of the hospital and thought about Captain Beefheart dropping out of the music business, moving to the desert and painting, and wondered how it applied to my job making roast beef sandwiches and wiping uneaten food off of plates. They told us not to feed potatoes into the insinkerator, so I threw a chili bowl into the spinning blades, just to see what would happen. The entire kitchen vibrated like an alien abduction roto-rooter stuck in a whale's asshole, and I watched the time-space continuum become dislodged, and start to reverse itself. I tried to calculate how many pieces of china I would have to feed into the machine to get me back to a point where I could feel. I didn't think the town's power grid would hold out.

A deformed man in a custodial uniform cleaning an unnatural amount of puke from a hallway broke my reverie. "I can't remember who got blamed for the Princess Di assassination," the janitor told me. The puke smelled like candy corn and ammonia. "I think the Mossad got the blame, but we all know ConAgra foods did it. I don't have proof, but it just feels right, you know?" He wore Halloween makeup — Dracula lipstick, zombie face paint, Frankenstein's monster stick-on neck bolts — and tried to look sexy with it, like a Dead Can Dance drag queen. I thought it distracted from the janitorial work, the pure craftsmanship involved in mopping down a vomit spill, spreading the puke sawdust, applying the pink germicidal spray cleaner. He seemed happy, or at least more happy than I was at the moment.

* * *

The phone echoed hold music on speaker, while an hours-long marathon of stupid clip shows echoed in the background, late on a Tuesday night. *Industrial Robot Disasters Caught on Tape* was the ambient soundtrack for my panic state, because I was too lazy to pick up the remote and change the channel. The robo-call would confirm the execution schedule, or announce it was pushed another 48 hours. They liked to schedule their killings to knock the latest scandal out of the news cycle, and the Assistant Governor just got caught having butt-sex with a dead illegal school-teacher, so I figured it would be a go.

But the robo-call didn't simply spit out the pertinent information I needed; it first played an ad for a 90-minute VHS tape of Randy Savage taking a massive dump. I mean, it's not one dump; it's like three or four spliced together with a bunch of retrospective footage, and the play-by-play is done by Mean Gene Okerlund. $99, or three easy payments of $49. And Okerlund refers to Machoman as his close, personal, long-time friend 168 times, too.

* * *

You read the only magazines you can find, *Vibe For Pregnant Teens* and *Country Shitkicker Kitchen*, while the guards get the man from the insides of the prison to the visiting room. I would have killed for an issue of *Juggs*, or even *Us Weekly*. You expect the maximum security facility to look like the pit where they keep Hannibal Lecter behind plexiglass at the Baltimore State Hospital for the Criminally Insane, but it resembles an elementary school built in the Eighties, the kind with open rooms and no sharp corners, and big, round sinks like fountains you operate with your feet, that utopian element of bizarre ergonomics that never quite caught on outside of the EPCOT center. Add a ring of guard rows with shotgun slots for firing in teargas canisters during riots, and heavy locked doors to protect the minimum-wage employees from crazed and psychotic men, broken for life by their 50-year torture sentences for getting caught with two match-stick-sized rocks of coke. Schools and prisons are all built by the same lowest bidder, with identical lead paint and asbestos-stuffed walls. At least that's what the urban legends tell you.

Virgil earned the prison name of Poundcake, even though he'd never been raped in the showers. The nickname alone is hazing enough to keep him just a hair's width outside of sanity. You ask him why he killed her, the basic Q&A for your dissertation. "She was the kind of bitch that lived for pregnancy scares and high drama. Fucked her with three condos and she still said they all broke. Gave her six bills to hoover out the little fucker, and she used the abortion money to go swim with manatees in Florida. Posted the shit on Facebook and everything. So I say to myself, either I put a gun in her mouth, or I watch her fake breast cancer and make mad bucks online. The judge didn't buy it, though. Fucking Obama."

Before prison, before the girl, when I first met Poundcake, he started getting obsessed with tradwives and the prepper lifestyle, to the point where he dressed like a Mormon housewife, with a horrible synthetic wig and the weird underwear under a bad dress. By the beginning of junior high, he started skipping classes every day to hide in the attic of his mom's house, hoard five-gallon buckets of gruel and make horrible TikTok videos about baking and scrapbooking while waiting for the apocalypse.

His attic was lined with that Owens Corning pink fiberglass insulation, which tore apart his skin like a chemical warfare weapon every time he hid up there. And modern scrapbooking paper bought at Hobby Lobby contains so many chemicals and post-recycled waste, it turns brown and disintegrates and gets eaten alive by dust mites in a matter of months, causing a low-key immune disorder. The poor fuck ended up spending two semesters in the lockdown ward of the local children's hospital, hooked on oxycontin for insulation exposure, babbling incoherent conspiracy theories about how the Ball corporation got out of the canning industry to become a military contractor and support the New World Order by building black helicopter parts. He got off oxys by smoking hashish his uncle brought back from 'Nam, but liked to dabble in schedule-ones after that.

Now, twenty years later, the cycle repeats, the same madness, a different plastic window and intercom system, a different end game. You talk about nothing, about sports and which neighbors have fallen down the drug k-hole, have ended up in other prisons for stealing copper wire or killing people at Black Friday sales. He asks for a Satanic Bible, but you can't get it past the guards. You promise to mail him a cake with a bottle of your aunt's Percocet baked into the center, but you know it won't get there on time. You think his death will be a huge thing, like when they fried those

Lindbergh baby guys, but the state kills people more often than Gucci Mane drops new albums. Virgil's death got a single line on the news pages, and it got pushed out of circulation when Kim Kardashian tweeted that she liked coffee enemas. You think death would bring closure, but like every other thing in life, it doesn't.

You leave, and stumble through the streets of a previous era, a different city, another case of horrific digestive system failure. Your rental car looks like every other car, and you think you parked it by a Chinese restaurant, but it's Chinatown and everything is a Chinese restaurant. Every car is the same, every restaurant is the same, every existence is the same. You consider ditching your entire life, maybe starting over, spending another ten years in school, becoming an autistic biologist who sits around slicing up brains and mounting them on slides, anything that doesn't involve people or talking. Poundcake is a metaphor for the voice in your skull telling you everything is wrong, nothing is worth living. Even after he is no longer alive, the metaphor remains.

The Form of the Honeycomb Cereal Sword

Every night, I drove into the hills on the old Suzuki motor-cycle, trying to escape something, everything. I'd enter a dark curve at top speed and the bald tires would skid side-ways on the asphalt, throwing me to the pavement, scraping my skin and teeth into dust and blood. I would lose the mo-torcycle in a chasm, and walk miles home, bruised, battered, and fucked. I'd search every cabinet and drawer in my apartment for analgesics, painkillers, distractions, ripping through empty cardboard boxes of codeine pills, hoping for the one last fix that I'd never find. Then I'd spend the next day in a cab, driving through the mountains, searching for my piece of shit bike, running up a huge meter while some dude that smelled like ass sweat and curry bankrolled his opium habit on my credit card. I don't read Susan Sontag or know what the fuck I'm talking about, but this was a metaphor for my life, I guess.

I thought by this point in history, government spy satel-lites and digital wiretaps would have online dating down to a science. Enter a valid PayPal login, throw your ideal breast size into the series of tubes, and a supercomputer in Palo Alto would sift through the data and find the perfect match.

I mean, Amazon already knows I want to buy books on paint huffing and Satanism without me telling them a thing. Jeff Bezos probably knows the exact time I will die. But add the human element, and everything goes sideways. No matter how much money I dumped into the Forever Alone personals, they always matched me with the perfect nightmare, and I came back for more every time.

The last candidate brought me to the movie *Love, Actually* on the first date, which tells you everything you need to know about that disaster. A Supreme Court judge's daughter and over-enthusiastic anorexic, she initiated phone sex with me on the fourth call, screaming "FUCK MY ASS! FUCK MY ASS!" into the receiver while I stroked it like a madman. 1-900 numbers will bankrupt you; always take advantage of a situation to save money on masturbation. She later hinted that my meager sexual history could be a deal-breaker, like my dozen conquests in a dozen years was akin to barebacking a porn star without a condom. Meanwhile, she fucked every FacePlace friend request she got during our courtship, and posted graphic details of her encounters online, which I only found after it ended, during the regret/shame phase of the cycle.

On a long and overdrawn second date at her place, I dropped the hammer, and told her there was no way I'd date someone two train connections and a shuttle bus away. She filled my voice mail with screaming diatribes every day for a month, telling me I gave up obligation-free anal and the greatest set of fake tits this side of the Mississippi. I didn't disagree, but sometimes you just don't stick your dick in crazy.

* * *

This was far from my first total failure at classifieds. When I was nine years old, I won a Japanese seppuku sword. It was in a Honeycomb cereal contest — not the one where they gave out the metal license plates, though. They used to award BMX bikes to the winners, but they switched for a year, to ceremonial Japanese disembowelment. It probably involved a lawsuit, maybe somebody linking Huffy bikes to ritual Satanism. I mailed in the winning game piece, a Keith Haring-designed illustration of the World Trade Center rendered as twin uncircumcised penises ejaculating on a flying saucer, and hoped for the best.

After six months of wondering if this was an elaborate scam, a generic brown box showed up via UPS, covered in Asian printing and strange shipping information, beaten apart and crushed on its transit halfway across the globe. Inside, wrapped in Tokyo newspapers, was the perfectly-forged saber. I spent most of the fourth grade slicing open every watermelon I could find. The razor-sharp blade passed through produce like Taco Bell runs through someone with colitis.

Then *Evil Dead* came out on VHS, and I got bored of all that ninja shit. It was all about chainsaws, shotguns, and demonic raping trees. The Japanese sword collected dust in the back of my closet, along with my tap-dance shoes and a chrome-plated trombone I bought at a yard sale and never touched.

In college, I needed money to score cough syrup and fix my custom lawn mower. (This was the summer when mowers were huge, right after that Tom Cruise movie about tractor racing, with all the Toro product placement.) I listed the sword in the free paper, and got about ten calls a week. Everyone was like "it's OK, but $2500 is too high for a 16th-century Koto sword. Would you take an out-of-state check for $5?" And then they would no-show.

On Friday, Dwight came over, a guy who called nine times a week about the sword. He wore a sweaty Kenny Loggins shirt, and drank warm egg nog in the middle of June. He looked like if David Lee Roth was never famous, and worked in a tire shop. He licked his fingers and ran them down the edge of the blade, then tasted the steel with his tongue.

"My jam is doing surgical procedures on dudes in an articulated city bus."

"The ones with two pieces, hinged together like an accordion?"

"Yeah! If you do surgery in a state-funded vehicle, you're immune to class-action lawsuits. But I only do it in the back half, dig? You get too much noise from bus radio in the front."

He hefted the blade a few times, did some Bruce Lee moves, and chopped off a blade on my ceiling fan. "It feels off. I'll give you a hundred bucks, cash. And a spear gun. You need a spear gun? I've got a buddy from 'Nam who drop-ships them from China. Damn nice spear guns."

"We live in Indiana. Why do I need a spear gun?"

"If you appreciate the fit and finish on a quality close-quarter underwater weapon, you'll need this spear gun." He pulled a thick wad of damp bills from his pocket, licked his fingers again, and counted off a hundred bucks in ones and fives. "Seriously, you will wonder why you ever didn't have a spear gun."

I took the money, but regretted it later. A few years after Dmitri Young retired from baseball, he beheaded his neighbor, and ninja swords became huge. And I never got that spear gun, either.

* * *

Decades later, round 422 on the dating site: she brought me to a restaurant in a medieval castle, a gothic diner with a dreary interior and a waitress that looked like Hubert Humphrey in drag who spoke no English. The Dark Ages restaurant's laminated menu was a bound book as thick as a Gutenberg bible, printed in impossibly small type. It was like reading ten David Foster Wallace books just to get through the appetizers. Unless you opened to a random page and pointed, you'd spend months trying to decide on a main course. When that business model failed, the restaurant landed a reality TV gig with that Gordon Ramsay rip-off who came in, yelled at the employees, slapped on a coat of new paint, and tried to flip around the business. The British food star's brain exploded in a massive aneurysm on camera, shooting blood out of his head holes like a bad death in an 80s Troma film. The Food Network had to abandon the rest of the season for hastily-assembled clip shows. Until then, she-Humphrey took our orders wrong, and left me to fend through the first date preliminaries.

My match was a slightly narcoleptic social worker or insurance agent or something involving paperwork and fatalities. Imagine a young Sally Struthers, without the satisfaction of feeding the orphans, stuck in a dead-end government job and obsessed with unicorns. She ordered fried sausages, breaded ham dipped in a french fry basket, soggy onion rings blackened by never-changed oil, and kept asking me inane questions, if I believed in ghosts, angels, UFOs, Jesus. I told her I thought Elvis was a lie made up by the CIA to sell us more food, and changed the subject, mentioning the latest Amanda Bynes meltdown, in which she ate a live goat at the MTV awards, screaming "drink the blood!" at the paparazzi. It was the cover story in the latest Us Magazine, which I skimmed through at the drug store checkout the day before. I don't normally follow the star gossip stuff, but it was better than silence or conversation.

An armed guard stood at the front door, next to the gum ball machines, strapped with a chromed Uzi, a walkie-talkie on his belt tuned to a horse racing channel. He read an *Archie* comic and laughed, ignoring the skinheads beating the shit out of an elderly barbershop quartet in the parking lot. He recognized my hell, the blind date scenario quickly catching fire like a Pinto with a bad gas tank in a rear-end collision. He didn't even have the common courtesy to hit me in the head with a brick.

"Do I look like what you thought I would?" she asked. I picked at the hash browns with a plastic spork, and tried to think of a way to dodge the trick question, but couldn't. When her profile said her hair was red, I thought she meant chick-from-*Mad Men*-with-huge-tits red, not blonde with a hint of red if you looked at it under a blinding klieg light. I didn't say anything, grunted a vague affirmative. She kept telling me I should smoke more pot, that it would heal my depression. I think she wanted me to buy her pot. I didn't want to buy her the onion rings.

I paid for both meals with a bad check, and planned my escape. I smelled like the frizzled oil that soaked through my clothes, into my skin, felt myself slipping into a high-carb coma, and wanted nothing more than twelve hours of black-out sleep in my own bed, but she insisted on a nightcap. She rode bitch on the Suzuki, and we went back to her apartment. It was a strange townhouse built in the Seventies by drug addicts with a *Brady Bunch* obsession: too much wood trim, spiral staircases running nowhere, and a kitchen full of rotting vegetables. It reminded me of a playable deathmatch level in one of the *Call of Duty* versions, and I immediately started scanning for the best place to camp with a sniper rifle. Her neighbor, who looked like Sammy Hagar with no teeth, sat on the front porch, prying dead rats from giant wooden traps. "They died for Jesus," he told us on the way in. "Jesus fucking hates rats. They can burn in hell."

Inside, I overlooked the extensive collection of Bryan Adams bootlegs that made up her entire CD collection, ignored the devout adherence to Ayn Rand coloring books, and sidestepped her somewhat contradictory love for government cheese, and the need to stockpile it by the fifty-pound box in a chest freezer underneath her lofted bed. When you haven't been laid in months, even a strong pulse becomes an option rather than a requirement. I tried to listen to her talk about the TV show *Northern Exposure* for hours, but kept getting it mixed up with *Twin Peaks*. I didn't own a TV at the time, and only vaguely heard about either show.

By some miracle, I remember a set of open-ended questions I memorized that could be applied to anything, from a Dale Carnegie wannabe that ran seminars at the local Jiffy Lube on Saturdays. Years ago, I bought an "increase your word power" cassette set along with a regular oil change for

$39, and he threw in the "feign interest" cheater card for free. I stumbled through the conversation prompts as we drank warm Bartles and Jaymes, and waited for the magic to happen.

She brought me upstairs, and stripped off her sweaty, smeg-encrusted clothes while I tried not to watch. Before the lights went out, I saw a giant bottle of lube on her night-stand, the five-gallon size, like the kind you use to fix tractor-trailer engines. It sat next to a giant roll of condoms, a thick coil like a belt of ammunition for the machine gun in the wing of a P-51 fighter plane. It looked like she stole them from a free clinic, the kind of generic, plain white wrapper, no-name rubbers that would break apart like one-ply toilet paper in scalding hot water. I planned on wearing ten.

The echo of a new age album full of off-key harmonic dissonance on her clock radio reminded me of a time a century before when the ideality of a life ahead of me kept me from slitting my wrists on a daily basis. I thought if I did the work, kept grinding it out, I'd stumble into an ideal relation-ship, an ideal career, a life that could be summarized in a sentence to any sitcom-watching idiot, and that would be that. But life isn't a problem you solve; it's a series of blank slates, 24 hours to the day that you choose to fill with life or shit. And when every person around you does nothing but hand you shit, there's this strange fluke in human nature, at least in my broken brain, that makes it seem ideal to accept those piles and packages of shit and say "of course this is mine." It's how I think and what I deserve, or so I've been conditioned to believe.

She assumed the position, but her ass smelled like rotting Taco Tuesday shit in a neglected infant's diaper, so I jerked off in the dark while she watched, and shot onto the headboard above me. She fell asleep and snored, and I stared at the ceiling, a sloped roof at an extreme angle, with a little window, a mothership moon bubble portal that looked out at the stars and flickered with the moving branches above the house. It gave me an intense flashback to one of the *Myst* video games, which I once played on an ancient Macintosh with a one-button mouse the size of an extra-large chimichanga at one of those "burritos as big as your head" taco trucks. But then I remembered it wasn't the game I remembered, but rather a fragment of *Twin Peaks*, the wind in the trees. My déjà vu was as manufactured as the wood used to panel the shitty old apartment.

I worried about the practicalities of getting to work the next day, so far removed from the years-ago college days of one-nighters and stumbling to class on no sleep and no shower, now living in a professional world of early office hours and khaki pants and bosses and pensions and insurances. I considered leaving early, making the jump for the door, leaving behind my clothes and riding my beaten Suzuki home naked, thankful I didn't have to chew off an arm like a wolverine in a steel trap. Instead, I stayed awake all night, watching the leaves and trees move in the darkness, deafened by her snores. Nobody would know my great shame and weariness, a regret even stronger than that of trading a vintage Japanese sword for a nonexistent spear gun.

Frankie Two Balls and the Catskill Zombie Drug Rehab Castle Fire

The old Armenian guy on the infomercial for Florida real estate blaring out of my TV said "Fo shizzle! Fo shizzle!" over and over. A 1-900 number scrolled across the screen, along with a series of warnings, like "NOT FDIC INSURED" and "MAY CAUSE RECTAL BLEEDING." The text looked like it was generated with a Commodore VIC-20, and the color balance and distortion of the video signal was about to induce a seizure in me, but I couldn't not watch, even as my apartment building burned to the ground.

I'd just binge-watched 68 hours of the Winter Olympics because of some amateur figure skater I wanted to fuck, and it became so unbearable, it required me to slam my dick in a toaster oven and burn down the entire housing complex. (I mean, allegedly. I didn't do it. There's no evidence.) Things like this happen sometimes, especially when you're watching the Ladies' singles ice skating event, as announced by Joe Buck, while blackout drunk after slamming two bottles codeine cough syrup and snorting an indeterminate powder you got from the middle of the desert years before.

The cable to the TV went out, probably melted in the flames. I grabbed a two-liter of throwback Mountain Dew soda and stumbled outside to yell at the first responders. "We didn't defeat communism in a proxy war costing a trillion dollars to deal with this shit," I said to a Michael Rapaport-looking firefighter who played *The Legend of Zelda: Spirit Tracks* on a Nintendo DS as the firestorm engulfed the entire neighborhood. The cocktail of opiates and chemicals surged through my bloodstream, and I knew I'd someday get pancreatic cancer and/or have a seizure while in line at a Popeye's chicken from my rampant cough syrup abuse. "This isn't about arson firestarting to achieve an erection — it's about the ethics of arson firestarting to achieve an erection journalism! You feel me, bro?"

The fireman half-grunted to agree with my tirade, then pocketed the handheld game console and left to try to fuck one of the spray-tanned, big-haired Long Island sluts who inevitably hung out anywhere it might be possible to blow a fireman or police officer. The fire continued to burn, and I breathed the fumes and dust, hoping to either get high or inhale enough asbestos smoke to end my horrible imprisonment on this shit planet. Neither happened.

* * *

Fire was not new to me. A decade before, maybe two, I took an extended family vacation to the Catskills for the dope-shooting season. My folks weren't into smack, but they couldn't pass up a good deal, and the mafia was giving junkies seven days for the price of five, plus a free book of coupons that were essentially worthless, but my dad kept insisting that we'd go bobsledding in July because it was four for the price of three.

My parents were fiercely anti-vacation for most of my childhood. When I was seven, my father won an AM radio contest, something involving John Sebastian, the song "Do You Believe In Magic," and a chainsaw. Our family got shipped off on a one-way voyage to a mysterious island in the Pacific, a place with hot temperatures, human cannibalism, and absolutely no TV reception. The natives there shoved bamboo reeds into their anuses, slowly enlarging them in hopes that the mighty cargo planes of World War 2 would return with refrigerators, canned meat products, and some VHS tapes of old NHL games. They never did, of course, and most of the men died young from terminal prostate infections.

While there, I lived in a battered quonset hut, learned braille (many of the native tribesmen went blind drinking fatal brews made from kava plants and diesel fuel), and spent most of the third grade convinced various breakfast cereals were famous works of literature written by Filipino forced labor workers indentured by the Post cereal corporation. I became pen pals with a friend in Uruguay who taught me about Nazi UFOs and Shakey's pizza's secret black sites in Cuba, where banned chemicals were used to teach household pets how to play musical instruments, in anticipation of the invention of YouTube 22 years later. After this island misadventure, the only trips we took were to the mall to buy lawnmower accessories and Toughskins jeans, so the Catskills junket was a new and terrifying experience to me.

The stench of rotting flesh filled the air for the entire trip, like the smell of a slaughterhouse during the triple-digit temperature of a heatwave. Zombie-themed drug rehab boarding resorts tacked raw goat livers and decaying beef carcasses to old cabins, their staff driving around on motor-cycles, throwing machetes at peoples' heads. Pre-teen Jewish kids with rich parents and hard-ons for early Romero detoxed from heroin and chewed on the animal flesh until collapsing from trichinosis. Paranoid, affluent families in Queens or Long Island would send their city kids to the Scared Straight-style re-education camps, where they beat the shit out of patrons until they agreed that *Full House* was an awesome show and they would never listen to Suicidal Ten-dencies again. It was also unnaturally humid that summer.

My parents, fallen deep into a Borscht-belt k-hole long before the days when you could just look that shit up on YouTube, and dragged us to a motel that looked like the set of a horror film where an undead asshole in a mask chopped up everyone around when they tried to fuck. There was a pool, but you could practically see the chlamydia and tuber-culosis swimming in the water, under a thick layer of pond scum. There also was no cable, and this was years before widespread internet, like when portable computing consisted of loading a mainframe onto the back of a wide-load truck. I knew this would be a month of nightmares and misery, my Vietnam.

Our room lacked air conditioning, just a single nine-inch fan spinning at about three RPMs to barely stir the turbid air. I didn't have anything to do all day except sit outside and watch the unbearable heat melt the roads. I compulsively reread the only book I had with me, a zine about the Japanese noise-core movement titled *High Volume Parametric Death Fucker*. It didn't even have much in the way of English prose, just poorly translated bursts of text that made no sense ("DEATH FUCK! DO IT BLENDER! FUCK DENTIST!"), and low-quality photocopies of rabid assholes driving a bulldozer through a club or playing a harp with their cock. It made more sense when you were dying of sunstroke, though.

This was also a horrible time in my late development, an era in which I was rapidly approaching the twisting forks into the road that defined adulthood. I felt like every decision in my life at that point was potentially world-killing. Like I'd spent nights in an insomnia daze, walking in the darkness, wondering if I would ever get laid and if I needed to find a college with a good bachelor's degree in feminist mortuary sciences, so I could declare a minor and score more chicks. I knew that I was making bad decisions in life, the kind of decisions that would haunt me forever, and I spent all my time in a deep, introspective funk, trying to wrestle with what to do. I was also at that crucial teenage stage where I needed to jerk off at least three times a day, and I couldn't get ten seconds of free time away from the family, so that wasn't helping things.

A man sat on a crate in front of the castle down the road. He looked like the Mexican Morgan Freeman, and drank from a bottle of furniture polish in a brown paper bag. "This is some real trench warfare bullshit," he said. "You here from that bullshit zombie thing down the way?"

I nodded. I'd walked to the fortress, hauling a huge jam-box, blasting a demo of Greg Ginn's punk harmonica album. The failed roadside attraction, the closest form of civilization to our camp site, was a stolen citadel, shipped over and reassembled brick-by-brick from Transylvania or Europe or Australia or one of those failed socialist countries that lost every major war of the last five centuries. I hoped the imitation pizza restaurant dungeon inside had anything to drink with ice in it.

The Mexi-Morgan guy talked about Morton Downey Jr's removed lungs, and asked passers-by for enough change to build a new shipping canal through the isthmus of Nicaragua. "Had a job as a jizzmopper on one of those Red Line all-porn double decker masturbation busses, until fucking Giuliani shut down the entire jerkoff bus industry. Lived with my brother for a while in Nebraska, until he got both of his legs cut off laying down on a railroad track in front of a Ralston-Purina supply train. He was protesting Bonz dog snacks because he wanted all dogs to be vegetarian. Kept saying Colonel Sanders went to the School of the Americas and got trained by the CIA to kill us all with chicken. Hand-to-mouth combat. Heart disease and minds. I think they're making a movie about it, but I haven't been to a theater since *Footloose*. Anything with tractor duels throws me, for some reason."

I bought the vagrant a shrink-wrapped club sandwich, along with my glass of ice containing a capful of Grape Nehi. He thanked me profusely, telling me three times that he prayed for the souls of the dead. I walked back to the motel, the gravel dust on the side of the road forming molten rivers of rock like the surface of Venus. I considered shoving the grape drink's quickly melting ice cubes into my ass, remembering an article about putting popsicles in your colon to combat heat stroke. I ate the cubes before I got the chance, though.

* * *

"You didn't give that asshole any money, did you?" My motel neighbor, Frankie Two Balls, waxed his white Caddy with a baby diaper. He was shirtless, tanned a nauseous bright orange, and wearing Andrew Dice Clay sunglasses. This was years before *Jersey Shore*, but Frankie was the same kind of prototypical Long Island/Jersey asshole, a thriving archetype that goes back decades. He'd later savor the rise of the guido stereotype, until he died of a massive coronary at age 47. (And I never asked him about the Two Balls nickname, because I didn't want to find out he used to have three balls and got cancer, or everyone in his family only had one, or what.)

I went back to my lawn chair of hell, and carefully traced the pictures of Mare Tranquillitatis onto my arm with a Sharpie. The photos taken from the Ranger 8 space probe served as a template for an intricate prison tattoo I planned for my next stint in an insane asylum. I'd later fill out the design with an improvised tat gun made from a disassembled Sony Walkman and some home-brew ink I fermented in the cell toilet. I'd do a stretch in the bin with the guy who later tattooed Mike Tyson's face, and he'd give me valuable pointers while I did a sixty-day hold for jerking off at a California Pizza Kitchen.

"You know there's bags of shit on the moon?" He stopped his daily car detailing job, and squirted Turtle Wax in his greasy Elvis hairdo, then licked his hands clean, like he'd just finished eating a plate of fifty hot wings. "Those moon guys, Lance Armstrong and Buzz Lightyear, they were up there and had to shit in Hefty bags. Then when they took off, they wanted to give a big 'fuck you' to the Russians, like so if they shot up a dude right after that, he'd get out of his rocket ship, and step in their shit. They probably tried to light the bags on fire before they blasted off, but they couldn't get it to work because, no air."

I felt like correcting him on the names, but Frankie Two Balls had a basic mental instability that made me want to not get involved. He once got banned from all Carvel's ice cream stands because he tried to fuck a Fudgie the Whale cake, but couldn't get it to melt enough to sodomize it.

"You wanna go into town later and bang out some whores?" He pronounced the word "hoo-as" and pumped his fist in the air. I declined. I could barely jerk off in the over-bearing humidity, let alone watch him try to procreate with the townies.

My parents would be gone for hours, watching some guy named Schecky or Schlomo slowly die at a place that looked like the set of *The Shining*. I'd read the article six more times about the guy from Osaka who stapled a rotary saw to his dick and called it art. The beggar would fall asleep and somebody would light him on fire and burn down the castle, which I guess was the point of the flashback, but now I'm regretting I didn't take a picture of that fire, photoshop in a church steeple, and use it for a black metal album cover.

Someday This Could Be You

I'm listening to Satanic black metal on a Sports Illustrated cassette walkman and watching the Indianapolis 500 on a Magnavox portable black and white TV in the garage. My mom made a yellow coffee cake out of Folger's and South American uranium, and it tastes like shit, but I've still eaten four pieces. My family is glued to the set, taking the race far too seriously. I'm rooting for a multi-car crash. This was years before Dale.

Our neighbor, a drunken garden gnome salesman, stumbles into the garage. He's filling his pockets with cake and trying to sell my Uncle Judas an ornamental mirrored globe. Judas won't buy anything, because he's an Amish-Satanist and can't touch money. He also got fired from Burger Chef two years ago for taking a dump in the salad bar.

"My daughter's going to major in dollhouse architecture," the neighbor tells my uncle. "I'm gonna have to send her money until she's 38. All I do is sell lawn jockey statues to old racists and fuck strangers through glory holes. My wife is addicted to Pampered Chef and my dog joined Scientology. My life is a fucking cliché. I'm ten minutes from buying a Corvette. You've gotta buy a gnome off of me."

He hands my uncle a picture of a stranger's cock pressed against a mirrored globe, then goes outside and lays facedown in the road to try and get a car to run him over. "Fucking end me!" he yells to everybody and nobody, tilting his head sideways to drink his Stroh's from a can in an "Is it Friday Yet!" foam cozy.

"What the fuck," I tell my uncle. "This subdivision has speed bumps every ten feet. The speed limit is like five miles an hour."

"He's drunk, his wife's leaving him for one of those Vegas acrobats that do all of the weirdo dances, and his daughter's some kind of freaky dollhouse architect. Let him sleep it off. Someday, this could be you."

He was right.

#JustKilldozer-Things

I had to wait for Fat Mike to finish taking a shit before we could go to the mall. His bowel movement ritual was an hours-long process, and I wished I would have brought something to read while I waited. I didn't want to be there waiting, but I didn't want to be in the Midwest in general. I had to travel back for the annual sorrow fest with the old people on the dirt farm. My long weekend was booked solid, shuttling between the various divorced and estranged pieces of the family who only communicated with each other through lawyers. I sacrificed my only few-odd-hour time slot to hang with Fat Mike, and he spent most of it in the bathroom unloading his bowels.

On the giant 80-inch plasma TV in his basement, I watched a CNN special report about the latest daily killing rampage. Grainy witness-shot camcorder footage showed a guy in a pumpkin-head costume furiously masturbating while driving a John Deere killdozer. Side-mounted flamethrowers took out cars and pedestrians, and lit the town's Christmas decorations on fire, enraging the War on Christmas crowd. Rooftop police snipers couldn't get a clear shot because of the pumpkin mask. The dozer's industrial-strength video projectors broadcast loops of *Full House* clips and anti-vivisection propaganda on the surrounding buildings. I mean, I didn't watch the guy because I was into him jerking off — no homo — but the carnage and devastation was astounding, and a bit motivating and inspirational. #JustKilldozerThings

Fat Mike burst from the downstairs bathroom fortress of solitude, blasting a can of Glade in each hand, laying down a heavy fog behind him like an Agent Orange cropduster blasting down a Cambodian jungle. He looked like the protagonist in a John Woo movie, bottles of air freshener akimbo. "God damn it, will you stop eating Wolf Blitzer's asshole so we can go already? We don't have all day to fuck around. Let's get some sluts and burgers."

"Am I driving us to this shithole? My rental car is full of Jolt cola. I'm trying to stockpile enough to get me through writing my next book. I think it's illegal in New York, or nobody gets it for some reason. Mafia-controlled soda distributors, probably."

"Fuck that, we can hoof it. Your car's going to get stripped clean in ten seconds flat if you leave it in that parking lot."

We walked through Mike's bombed-out subdivision. The donut effect of white flight and gentrification was in full swing; the old ring around the city filled with baby boomer tri-levels, like Fat Mike's place, were left abandoned as the old people fled to the far outer suburbs to hole up and wait for the race war apocalypse. The inner city, once a total hellhole, was now taken over by artisanal vegan cupcake stores and gluten-free art galleries.

"Look at this shit." He pointed to a shotgun ranch with three dozen Confederate flags flying in the front yard. The chimneys of the shack house billowed with meth production byproducts. A sign made out of a sheet of plywood was nailed over the front door. Spray-painted on it was the simple universal message of "NO" and nothing more. It was probably all the residents could spell. "Everyone moved out because they were afraid of the apocalypse, but it already happened, years ago. The second they built that first Applebee's, civilization was over."

Our destination was the Checkers hamburger stand out past the ghetto mall that was days away from implosion and conversion into a stupid outdoor concept shopping center that nobody would shop at because people are too lazy to walk from store to store outdoors. Fat Mike knew some chick from his sociology class who worked at the burger place, and he was convinced if he ate there every day, within a month he'd be balls-deep in the cashier while she wore clown makeup with weights clamped to her tits and he played an import-only Pokemon game for the Nintendo DS she bought him. He tends to have unrealistic expectations of what he can get from women. That Nintendo game is impossible to find on eBay, at any price, and I wouldn't expect him to do anything involving weights.

We cut through the parking lot of the neighboring Wal-Mart, where a Mad Max caravan of beaten, decades-old RVs and burner school busses parked in a circle, a makeshift arena for to-the-death bum fights. People wagered Taco Bell gift cards and hand-written IOUs for contract killings and scatological rites, while two men dressed in adult diapers and chained together at the left wrist fought each other with a circular saw in their right hand. One of the drifters' kids recorded it all on a Nokia phone and posted clips on You-Porn. The quality wasn't great — even at high noon, the blinding sodium lights of the parking lot were brighter than the sun, so the video was mostly blurs, light trails, and camera shakiness. But you could hear the screams and the unmistakable sound of saws cutting flesh.

Past the caravan, we walked through the abandoned and bombed-out cars and garbage, toward the hamburger joint. If you needed to dump a few gallons of used motor oil, get rid of a burned-out big-screen CRT TV, or ditch a corpse, this was the place. Security was nonexistent, and unless you woke up somebody living in an immobile RV, nobody was looking.

"Hey man, doesn't this remind you of that encampment in *They Live?* Like where everyone crashed out in downtown LA or whatever? Fuck California, man."

"You know that movie was fake, right? I mean, Roddy Piper was in it, but it doesn't mean it's a documentary. And you think the coasts are bad, but seriously, fuck this place.

There's bodies hanging from trees, every car is a 4x4, and every building is a church or an illegal check cashing store and abortion clinic. This whole state is like one of those common core math problems where four equals seven. It makes no logical sense."

Fat Mike's female prospect was not on duty when we arrived at the restaurant. I use the term "restaurant" loosely, because this was a primitive drive-in place with limited seating, which was all outdoors and covered in human shit. We ordered a brace of high-fat food, everything covered in bacon and mayonnaise. We also got large 64-ounce pails of ice and brown flavorless water, apparently caused by a shortage of soda syrup. Fat Mike pitched his drink at the passing traffic in anger, hitting a Miata convertible and causing it to screech off-road and almost run over a meth addict dressed as the Statue of Liberty standing outside a cash-for-gold place.

We collected the dripping paper sacks of greasy burgers and fries from the walk-up window and then found another concrete picnic table in a junkie park across the street from a Home Depot, a place grudge-built by the retail chain to keep illegals and homeless off the store property. A drug dealer sold dollar crank and watched a battery-powered TV plugged into a boosted cable signal, the coax strung down from the apartments next door.

"You guys want to score?" He pulled out a Minions lunchbox filled with little plastic baggies of powder that looked as coarse as rock salt, but with more impurities.

"We're good, man. Any news on the killdozer?"

"He took out another taco truck. They think he's anti-immigrant now. I think he just hates trucks."

"I just hate," Fat Mike said.

"Well, let's be grateful you can't weld armor onto your riding lawn mower," I said. I unwrapped a double burger, and looked under the soggy bun for any hidden pickles, because fuck pickles. "Why do you keep eating this garbage? I'm getting an ulcer just smelling this."

"Dude, pussy. She's not here today, but I'm wearing her down."

"You had a sure thing going with that blue-haired cashier at the Sunoco station out on the 33 bypass before you fucked it up." The Sunoco girl was a few years younger than us, maybe a freshman when we were seniors. She was a bit slow, maybe boring, but looked marginally okay. I hoped if Fat Mike locked into some kind of regular fuck thing and shacked up with a member of the opposite sex, he'd become slightly domesticated, maybe shower more often, and stop dragging me on epic voyages to horrible strip clubs where we had zero chance of anything ever happening, other than great financial loss and airborne weaponized strains of STDs not even known yet to civilians.

"Yeah, I wanted to get a second date with her, because she said she had irritable bowel syndrome. I thought maybe she'd be down with butt stuff, you know, because of all the enemas and colonoscopies and shitting her pants. But she ghosted the fuck out on me, never returned my calls. I think she's a lesbian or something."

"Dude you put a gun in her mouth at a Starbuck's and started screaming at her about Superman comics. I doubt she's calling you back. She probably swore off phones for the rest of her life. You're goddamn lucky she didn't call the cops and get an assault charge on you. They can haul you into court for leaving a sarcastic comment on a chick's Instagram photo these days. Your little stunt could get you indefinitely detained at a CIA black site in some country with ten umlauts in its name."

"She fucking said she didn't watch Spider-Man and Superman movies! Her movie preferences are wrong, and she's mixing up Marvel and DC universes. Superman can't appear in a Spider-Man movie, so she should have said 'Spider-Man or Superman movies.' What the fuck was I supposed to do?"

"Maybe you could stop brandishing a concealed firearm on first dates. And keep your dick in your pants."

"I didn't even take my dick out! I was saving that for after she paid the check."

Fat Mike ate his nacho pizza burger like an apex predator tore apart carrion, pieces of bacon and melted cheese flying in every direction. I tried to think of what apex predators I'd actually eaten. It sounds horrible, like maybe I'd spent time making dolphin burgers and lion pizza, but technically grouper and tuna are apex predators, so it's a largely stupid mental game, and I drifted from that to useless 80s movie and video game trivia, as usual. (Apex predators reminded me of the movie *Predator*; because of Arnold, that reminded me of the movie *The Running Man*; that reminded me of the video game *Smash TV*; that reminded me of "I'd buy that for a dollar!"; that was from the movie *RoboCop*. Also, Dweezil Zappa was in *The Running Man*, and within two minutes, I'd be balls-deep in a remaster of *Trout Mask Replica*. Don't even ask.)

"Do you remember when they installed RoboCop in the police precinct and OCP put in that food machine and the one guy dipped his hand in it and he said, 'Tastes like baby food?'" I asked him. "Do you think RoboCop kicked his ass for putting his fingers in it? Can RoboCop catch a cold from double-dipping? Could an enemy design some rogue cold virus and take him out? Or does RoboCop have Alex Murphy's human immune system?"

"Stupifuck — they would give him vaccines. Cops and military have to take like fifty shots a year, even more if they go into combat. They have a lot of money invested in that project. Those scientist dudes are sitting there 24/7 watching him dream and shit. Don't you think they're gonna spend a few bucks on some vitamin C tablets and a flu shot?"

I think I lived on the cusp of the flu shot revolution, so I never thought about it much. The shots didn't exist when I was a kid, but now you can't go to a grocery store or dry cleaner without someone trying to jab a syringe of dead influenza cells in your arm or ass. I was driving on the toll road once and didn't have an E-ZPass. When I went through the cash-only lane and grabbed my paper ticket from the dude in the parka inside the little glass booth, he jabbed me with a needle. I blew through the gate like a *Starsky and Hutch* chase scene, totally fucked the rental car, shooting blood from this spike in my arm. I hope it was the fucking flu shot.

"I'm going to need a real drink," I said. "We need to brave that fucking Wal-Mart and see if they have any cold drinks in bottles. I can't deal with the failure of fountain soda."

"Fair enough. I might have an aftershit coming up after that earlier domination match. Let's see how bad their men's crapper looks."

We walked in the flickering fluorescent glow of the store, and I immediately saw an ex-girlfriend, four hundred pounds heavier, aged fifty years in the last ten. She pushed a cart filled with boxes of salt and vinegar douche, while twelve kids ran behind her, tearing open bags of candy and eating them like they were free entrees at a Vegas strip club. I did a drop and roll and hid behind a kiosk offering coffin and crypt services, available by mail at deep discounts. Why pay some shady local rack rate when you can get a cardboard sarcophagus for when they fish your nephew Ricky's bloated corpse out of the St. Joseph river and don't let you cremate it because of the amount of uranium impurities in his subcutaneous fat? That ashes-in-the-Ralph's-coffee-can trick only works in the movies. Premium finishes also available, ask about our organic bamboo models.

"Hey man, isn't that the chick who jerked you off in the parking lot of TGI Friday's back in 1994? Man, she looks fuckin' brutal now."

"Shut up. Make it go away. And it was Olive Garden. Free breadsticks and reluctant handjobs. It almost made up for the fact that every single thing on that menu makes me shit blood."

"Oh man, if I didn't still owe you 99 dollars from that Black Sabbath box set, I'd totally go over there and blow your cover. She looks like that bitch from *Misery* with a bad meth problem. Maybe you can get her to break your legs and rewrite the last half of your next book."

"Do not ever reference a writer who is a fan of the Red Sox again, or I will fucking end you."

Just seeing her reminded me of the abject failure of my life at the time, a complete shame spiral of thoughts about not only every interaction with her, but every moment of my existence in that era. I drifted through an absolute desolation before I met her, spending days, weeks not talking to a single human. I somehow managed to score a job doing technical support for a server farm that ran an online necrophilia forum, and nobody knew there was a customer service hotline. Or maybe they were too embarrassed to call when a server died. I spent most of my four to midnight shifts trying to cook lunchmeat on the ventilation holes of $600,000 mainframe computers, as well as snooping through user directories that were unlocked, to find anything interesting.

One time, I found this dumpy middle-aged librarian's email inbox, backed up to a file, accidentally copied to the / tmp directory of a Unix mainframe. I skimmed through it — she had good game, propositioning twenty-year-old guys with promises of alcohol and head. I read in fascination until she described a fantasy to a guy where he got his uncle to shave her back with a straight razor and apply various condiment packets (mayo, mustard, ketchup, hot sauce) to her freshly-shorn skin in a map of the continental 48 states. The subject line was "MY BODY IS READY." I never read the whole thing because my pastrami started burning on top of a VAX 6440 mainframe, and it lit off the halon fire extinguisher system in the machine room, spewing poisonous foam everywhere.

Fat Mike went to the gun section to look at crossbows, and I had no desire to hang out with a bunch of people stocking up on pork-dipped AR-15 ammo for the apocalypse. I crashed in a waiting chair in the maternity section and pulled out my iPhone to look for more killdozer updates. This part of the state had no LTE or 4G connectivity, and only a fleeting 3G signal existed a few blocks of the state capital. My Facebook app sat and spun, not giving me any information. The store had thousands of big screens on every wall, but instead of news or programming, they were all tuned to a sixty-second loop of an annoying cartoon with an anthropomorphic hot dog rapping about states' rights and why taxes are bad.

I gave up on current news and watched an East German soap opera I saved for offline use, a choppy soliloquy about work camps and beet paste in a German dialect I barely understood. The 320x200 video rip looked like it was transferred from tape to digital and back to tape again, swirling colors like a Skinemax feed going in and out of scramble. Jam the toothpicks of life into the metaphorical buttons of the cable box, and hope for a clear shot of tits and Seventies bush before that Scientific Atlanta melts and catches fire.

"We gotta go. Put that shit away and let's get the fuck out of here, pronto."

"What, did the food work through you that fast? Maybe just shit your pants and get it over with. You can buy a new pair of Wranglers for four dollars here."

"No, not that. Can you believe this piece of shit place won't sell me an AR-15 because I showed my dick to the cashier?"

"Why, do they have a maximum length for people buying assault rifles?"

"Just shut the fuck up and get us out of here before the cops show up."

We ran for the door, and Fat Mike threw a piece of a truck tire into a burning garbage barrel in the parking lot as a distraction tactic. It sent up a cloud of smoke like an airplane crash, giving us enough cover to run to a 7-Eleven down the road and stock up on caffeine and sugar to make it through the rest of the day.

"Hey chief, you know what happened to the killdozer?" Fat Mike asked the cashier, a guy who looked like Charles Bronson's fat brother who ended up working at 7-Eleven.

"Yeah man, he cut a deal with the hostage negotiators. The ratings were so high on the chase sequence, he brokered a seven-figure holding deal with HBO. Executive producer credit on whatever they develop, and all charges dropped. He said he wants to do the next *Daily Show*, but with tits."

"So look for *Killdozer* on HBO next year," I said. "What a fucking cash grab."

"America, what a country!" the cashier said, before going back to reading his porno mag.

I don't remember what we bought, but it was overpriced. The Checkers hamburgers made me shit blood for three days, and I had to take an entire box of Immodium before I could even dare to try my return cross-country flight. The drug dealer in the parking lot got his TV taken away by the cops. *Killdozer* got cancelled after three episodes. Fat Mike never fucked that girl. And I think they turned Checkers into Rally's or Hardee's or one of those other sub-par regional hamburger joints. What a country indeed.

It's Impossible to Learn to Flush Prosthetic Arms down a Toilet by Reading Books

The idea for a short film shot on Hi8 camcorders about the use of strawberry jam in Satanic rituals came and went in under a week, but not before I bought a thousand dollars of kit I never used. The UPS ground shipments arrived at work on a rainy Tuesday, boxes of grey-market Sony gear from Big Earl's Camera Land and Gun Emporium, the only place online you could buy both Canon SLRs and AK-47s. (I didn't buy an assault rifle; I shopped there because they were the only place online that would take American Express and not ship it to my apartment billing address, where UPS would leave it all out on the street and the boxes would be stolen within sixty seconds.)

As usual, the sudden desire to make documentary films had to do with a breakup. It was a soon-to-be-a-footnote, out-at-third-date thing where she kept asking me to hook her up with a copy of Windows Vista Ultimate Signature Edition.

After she dumped me, she went through a Sherman's march of dick, either in an effort to find herself, or as an affront to me, the ultimate revenge. She texted me a video of her jamming a safety pin in her clit, the Phil Collins song "Against All Odds (Take a Look at Me Now)" playing in the background. It disgusted me — not the safety pin part — but that song. Mariah Carey covered it for the album *Rainbow*, supposedly because of her breakup with Derek Jeter, and that bothered me even more, so I couldn't think about the trifecta (safety pin, Phil Collins, Derek fucking Jeter) anymore and I didn't jerk off for a week.

I set up an American Express cards' worth of video gear in my studio apartment and started recording a documentary about throwing things down my toilet while I drank codeine cough syrup. After a hundred hours of footage, I got the plumbing jammed on a fatal jag of lit-on-fire green army men, coated in Aqua Net hair spray. I still had a hook-up on the CFC-packed stuff from a place back in Indiana that bottled it for export to former Soviet regimes with no environmental laws. It looked like pure napalm on fire, albeit at the wrong scale for a good macro lens closeup. The documentary had some subtext about the war in Kosovo, mostly me yelling "Slobodon! Slobodon!" over and over as the toilet flushed.

(And I wasn't pro- or anti-Slobodon Milošević. I mean, anti-, sure, I'm anti-genocide and everything, but I'm also stupid and never follow the news. I mostly just had his name on my mind, like from an *SNL* sketch or comic strip appearance. It's like how sometimes I get the name Detlef Schrempf stuck in my head and can't stop saying it over and over. Detlef Schrempf. Detlef Schrempf. Detlef Schrempf. It won't go away. It's like Tetris syndrome, highway hypnosis, the song "It's a Small World." I don't even follow basketball. Detlef Schrempf. Detlef Schrempf.)

Living in a studio apartment with no working toilet had its disadvantages, although with a sink to piss in and a seventh-story balcony to let things fly, it almost worked. I made it about a week before breaking down and calling the front office. After an hour of Lionel Ritchie hold music, I got a maintenance call in to the building management, who was generally too busy slumlording to actually service the building.

The building's plumber was a greaser who looked like Ritchie Valens, had be been alive at the same time as Taco Bell's fourth meal era. He was on some rant about jojoba while he snaked out the toilet, then told me about how he was down to fuck women with big hair. The rant about Aqua Net and whores was more than worthwhile, but I was also fixated on the industrial-grade toilet maintenance equipment he was using. It was all stainless steel and looked like something H.R. Giger invented to fuck/kill an alien on the dark side of the moon.

"I wish it was still the 80s. I used to like Warrant, Bullet Boys — hell, I even liked that first Winger album. True story.

And I'd fuck out those chicks from Nelson." I wasn't going to interrupt this with the unfortunate fact that Nelson was two dudes; I just wanted to find a way to get the camcorder rolling again. "My wife found my porn collection, gave me an ultimatum: throw out my skin mags, or hit the road. I'm sleeping in the janitor's closet now. It's got my name on the door, what the hell. Mop sink to piss in. How many of these army men did you flush, anyway? Looks like you lost an entire battalion down the shitpipe."

* * *

I felt bad for the super, because I could sympathize. Not about the porno mags — I can't even pay attention to anything lower than 1080p-quality anymore. I mean the sanitation worker part. I used to clean MRI machines for minimum wage at a county hospital in Lebanon, Indiana. This machine was built for farm animals, with a table that could hold up to 800 pounds, so it attracted a lot of morbidly obese people who tend to shit and piss in the tube. I spent most of my time in elbow-length rubber gloves, spraying the machine down caustic pink industrial cleaner that would take the skin off a fried chicken in ten seconds flat. I got the cleaning job in hopes of getting a few hours of free use on the machine every week or two, for the typical MRI-your-junk scheme, but it never happened. Small hospitals always overbook the fuck out of their MRI, and this one was no exception.

I was on duty one day, and a freak circus got involved in a traffic accident, something with a church bus full of 28 homeschooled kids cutting off a clown car. They airlifted in the carny, a guy with head-to-toe tats for the band Reel Big Fish. He had a lame stage name, Insano the Clown, and thought he was edgy because he had both ears pierced, and could puke on command. This was before pretty much everyone under the age of 25 in the Midwest had full-body tattoos and multiple genital piercings, so the guy was somewhat unique. The fender bender screwed up his leg, a few torn ligaments, and he made his living running around like an idiot, something you can't do well on a cane. The insurance pre-approval went through, so they threw him in the tube, and lit it up for a knee series.

Here was the problem: Insano did some "after dark" shows at strip clubs, where he was Insano the Anal Clown. His big gimmick was putting stuff in his ass: ping pong balls, paddles, bowling pins, socket wrenches, flowers in vases, whatever you had handy. His specialty was chess pieces. He'd bring a chess set, shove all the pieces in his colon, and put the board on the stage. In a matter of moments, he'd shit out all 32 pieces, and land them on the board in various openings or endgames of famous matches. (There's a great YouTube video of him laying down the starting moves of every Bobby Fischer game from the '72 World Chess Championship. The anus itself is blurred out — YouTube terms of service, you know — but you can see him crouching over the board, and PLLLLBPT "it's a Spassky–Fischer, game 3 Modern Benoni Defence, Classical Main Line!")

Insano got really into metal chess sets, when the plastic ones weren't doing it for him anymore. And he must have forgotten a few pieces, because when they switched on that MRI, the 30,000-Gauss magnet fired up instantly, turning the metal chessmen in his colon into flying instruments of death. Those sharp-cornered rooks and bishops and kings tore through his intestines and guts from the inside out like a set of shark's teeth through chum. The horrified doctors turned off the machine after a few seconds, but the damage was done. He looked like he went ass-first into a chipper shredder, still alive, screaming, his bowels and their contents covering the inside of that Philips Intenia 3.0T machine.

It took me days to mop down the room, pieces of Insano's guts stuck to the floors, ceiling, every wall. It smelled like shit, booze, and circus food for weeks, no matter how much pink disinfectant spray I soaked everything with. I think they ended up scrapping the MRI machine, junking a three million dollar piece of medical equipment because some genius tattooed hipster with a bum knee had a chess set in his asshole. I later got fired for trying to fuck my boss's wife, and eventually found another job digging graves, a story I'll save for some other time.

* * *

I forgot to tell the super about the MRI incident, and remembered it hours later, on a random quest to find a Coke Zero Slurpee somewhere in the tri-state area. The rambling drive on the highway went for one side of the tape, the universal measure of time back when cassettes were a thing. Drive for 22 minutes, give or take, pointed north on a highway into nothingness, then flip the tape, turn the car around, head back. Reminded me of a time I got picked up hitchhiking by a woman who claimed she was going to climb Mount Rainier dressed as bigfoot. I don't remember why I was hitchhiking; either my car had broken down, or I was bored. Maybe both.

She wore hospital scrubs for a pediatric nurse, the kind with Spongebob Squarepants on them in a floral pattern, but with the front slit down so you could see some cleavage. I don't know if she was a nurse or pretended to be one so she could kill old people, but she did give me a bottle of this codeine-laced cough syrup that contained about 17 other anti-emetic and psychoactive chemicals.

We drove in the darkness and she told me about how she wanted to study dolphins, but I ignored her, trying to block out the Billy Joel album she played in the tape deck. *Glass Houses*, "All For Leyna" — it made me think about how two of Joel's bass players had died, and as a bass player listening to the bass line in a Billy Joel song, that worried me. Also, the nurse couldn't drive, swerving in and out of traffic, barely missing pedestrians and other cars, while telling me about how she liked Applebee's.

The syrup gave me horrific nightmares, like analingus-with-Ronald-Reagan-at-Red-Lobster horrific. Panic tremors permeated the multi-level terror depths, visions of porno-graphic fetus-murder cultists driving souped-up Camaros with their massive V-8 engines replaced with steam locomo-tive motors, blasting Bachman-Turner Overdrive and chug-ging Clamato that they would later vomit out of their car doors onto passing traffic. I woke and had to assure myself over and over that it was only a dream, which checking my teeth for any dental trauma.

* * *

"These army men are nothing," the super told me, pulling the debris out of the toilet. "Last week, I had to snake out a crapper for this insane Iraq vet down in #345. He flushed his artificial arm, I think on accident. Was on an oxy ben-der, and the VA's got him loaded up on Xanax and Ambien. He thought a *Space Invaders* game was one of those IUDs. Freaked out, drank four quarts of bleach mixed with Coca-Cola. I don't know how the arm got down the toilet — I learned not to ask questions a long time ago."

I thanked the super, then pressed Stop on the camera, rewound the tape for later review. I didn't think two hours of ass-crack footage would fit well into my overall vision for the doc, but maybe I could cut it down, run it through some trippy effects and use it as b-roll to cut into the scene when I blew up the entire building. I didn't know how I'd pull that one off, but I'd figure it out later, maybe.

Just Because You Got Gang-Fucked by the Cleveland Cavaliers in 1997 Doesn't Mean You Can Bring 19 Items to the Express Lane

A portly woman in a throwback basketball jersey hate-fucked a three-layer sheet cake in the express checkout line of the Fred Meyer, throwing packs of gum on the floor, screaming about the Cavaliers losing four games to the Pacers and how she allegedly had Shawn Kemp's abortion. Her elderly mom tried to pay for the whole mess with a food stamp EBT card that wouldn't go through the register. "Vitaly Potapenko still owes me fifteen dollars!" she screamed at the cashier. Her hair was nineties as fuck, a foot taller than her head, and she smelled like either car wax or Celine Deon cologne. Snot was running down her nose, onto a vintage Brevin Knight jersey, reducing its resale value considerably.

She looked familiar to me, maybe from my hours of clicking through online mugshots, looking for some free entertainment. Blogs were dead, Comcast wanted $800 a month for HBO and 600 other channels I'd never need, and even the free paper wasn't free anymore. Most mugshots in this state blended together, a perfect storm of obesity, meth scabs, and facial tattoos. But something seemed recognizable about her — maybe she was on COPS once. I intently watched the no-admission-charge cake-rape spectacle, waiting for the inevitable store security show-of-force overreaction, wishing I had a GoPro camera to document the beat-down.

My own cart had exactly 18 items: Fleet enemas, frozen generic burritos, Hungry Man TV dinners, and industrial-strength Immodium AD, in liquid formula that I could mix with Dr. Pepper. (The store-brand liquid contains alcohol too, which is a nice bonus.) The cart contents summarized my steady diet of starch, fat, and regret. I needed salvation, hope, and enough Hot Pockets to make it until payday. I did not need this woman rolling on the floor by the candy bar display, in either a demonic possession or drug overdose, screaming "FUCK THE PACERS!" waiting for somebody to mace her. You can't even go to the grocery store without getting PTSD. The food was bad enough; I'd ride the constipation/diarrhea rollercoaster for weeks after gorging through this latest load of frozen extruded tubes of death.

Two rent-a-cops with Tasers arrived, and the mom-and-daughter duo split, leaving behind a thousand dollars of perishables to rot. I made it to the front of the line and started emptying my items onto the spinning conveyor. The cashier was a chubby girl with glasses thicker than the Hubble space telescope's primary lenses and skin pocked with acne scars like the dark side of an asteroid-beaten moon of Saturn. She had a nice rack, but no self-confidence, and the vacant stare of someone who spent too much time idolizing the inane.

As she shuffled my conveyor belt items over the electric eye of the laser scanner, she saw my t-shirt, which was some garbage I got for free when I bought a Marshall tube amp I ended up selling at a loss when I realized I'd never really learn to play guitar. "I'm really into TubePunk," she said. "I only buy electronics made with valves. I want to buy an ENIAC iPhone. It takes up two buildings, but it's so retro, it's awesome. Valves rock."

"What the fuck do you mean valves? Like the video game company, or the piece of plumbing?"

"No, you know, what British call vacuum tubes. UK people are so dreamy. I love their accents — I wish I could visit there someday. *Doctor Who* and cars driving on the wrong side of the road — and fish and chips. I love Eddie Izzard, too. I talk to this guy on IRC, and..."

I hope this bitch finishes cashing me out before she starts talking about U2, I thought. I imagined her talking me into paying $900 to go to a conference at a fungus-infested convention center south of the airport to brave a sea of neckbeard dorks lined up to see a guy who wrote Star Trek fan fiction and watched Wil Wheaton take a shit back in 1996. Regardless, I'd ask for her phone number and probably spend the first three dates listening to her ramble on about Bono and Monty Python.

* * *

Paid, bagged, and clear of the misery inside, I headed through the airlock doors to see if my car was still outside. In the vestibule between doors, there was a parking area for 64 motorized carts, each with a charger cord. All 64 units were currently in use, circling the frozen dessert aisle at low speed. While I was doing my big loop earlier, a cluster of battery-powered mobility tanks were log-jammed in the meat and fat aisle, their users beating each other with hand combat weaponry like flails and blackjacks. It was a beginner's mistake to even try navigating through the freezer cases that had bulk fried chicken nuggets and corn dogs. It was like trying to get to the exit of a Who concert at Riverfront Coliseum.

I found the quick path through the store, the not-soda, not-beer beverage aisle, which was labelled "'New Age' Bullshit Drinks," where everything was covered in a half-inch of solid dust. "Water is for communists and subversives," said a stock boy, an idiot in coke-bottle glasses hunched over a display of canned bacon, clacking at the containers of pork lard product with a price gun. "Drink beer or get the fuck out of the store."

"What if I was an alcoholic?"

"Then get the fuck out of the store!" He pointed the price gun at my head, as if it shot full metal jacket rounds instead of little orange stickers with purple-stamped prices. "'What if I was an alcoholic?' Get the fuck out of here! Are you some kind of cop? GET THE FUCK OUT!"

* * *

I got home, filled my freezer with food, then immediately regretted every purchase and left the house to get some pizza. There was a place down the street that had a decent pie at a cheap price, so I ducked in for a few slices. Their sign said "Pizza As Thick As Your Dick!" in Comic Sans, with a bunch of Minions characters around the edges. But they served cold Corona in bottles, so what the hell.

The inside of the restaurant smelled like burned crust and stale beer, sporting the usual wooden decor of any pizza joint in the deep Seventies, with chalkboard menus and promotional beer neon signs flickering on the walls. The cashier looked like she was a high school cheerleader who peaked ten years ago, with a hundred thousand miles of dick on the odometer, beaten down by life and working for tips in a place that didn't even grate their own cheese. Solid, just my jam.

"I'll take the stuffed Colon Blow with pepperoni, and FUCK OLIVES. And a pitcher of Pepsi, no ice." I decided against the beer because I didn't want that Minutemen song stuck in my head all day. She sighed, keyed the order into an ancient NCR register with a nixie tube display from 1973. Cash only, the paper stuck to the grey plastic machine said. I unfolded a twenty, got my change and left the coins and a couple of bucks in the beer pitcher with a "TIPPING IS NOT A CITY IN CHINA" sign on it, handwritten in that annoying sorority Sharpie lettering.

I nabbed a wooden table in the front of the restaurant. It wobbled, and was covered in ten thousand coats of polyurethane, a thick fake-plastic varnish layer that could have contained fossilized ferns from the Jurassic era. The Ad Sheet I grabbed from a wire stand at the front door only served as a distraction for three minutes, the time it took to find the hooker ads in the back all contained moon-faced stock art whores printed at like 9 DPI, resembling topographic maps of Mars with fake tits.

Through the front window, a scene unfolded at the bong shop located next to an Indian garment store called "Sari Charlie." A woman dressed in two pieces of thread fashioned into a bikini held a sign saying "MANDATORY SUICIDE 5$" and jumped up and down, bobbling her fake double-D bags. Cars skidded off the road, hitting fire hydrants, driving into storefronts, and taking out pedestrians. Next to the bong shop, in a dirt pit, two guys in wife-beater shirts collected money, shot people in the back of the head, and dumped the corpses in the pit.

"Hey man, you think those are real?" A guy who drank too much Mountain Dew and still believed in professional wrestling brought my microwaved pizza to the table. It smelled wrong, like a scratch-and-sniff sticker of a pizza, not an actual pizza. "She looks like that reporter on NBC-7, with the helmet hair. Nicer rack, though."

"All reporters have that helmet hair. There's a factory in Flint, Michigan that installs it. They used to make the tail fins for Cadillac sedans, moved into hair after Ralph Nader fucked over the auto industry. And those pant suits will hide anything. She could have a set of centipede arms under there, for all we know. Is the pizza here any good?"

"I eat it. But no. You might want to go across the street and blaze one first. There's a guy who works there named Carlos, who can hook you up with an MJ card if you don't have one. Tell him you have brain fog. I think that's a medical thing. Or maybe scurvy."

"I'm good, thanks." I had no need for overpriced, lab-grown frankentrees, especially if I needed to pay a weed doctor with a fake internet degree from Costa Rica $200 to get a club membership that expired in a year. Drugs are only punk rock when they're illegal. Fuck this safety shit — takes the fun out of everything. Give me some hash that may or may not be dipped in pure angel dust and smuggled in some mule's asshole that will make me try to fuck a cop car. We die like real men here.

I examined the food carefully for spit or roaches, and it looked okay, despite the smell. The last time I ate a stuffed pizza, we were trying to send a RoboCop into space to fight the alien hordes, and protect us from de-orbiting space garbage. Not NASA — they don't do shit anymore, except send obsolete cameras that don't even belong on an Android phone to planets with nothing to see except grainy dirt. I'm talking about my roommate Wayne, who started his own space program part-time. He also worked as a delivery driver for Sloppy Seconds pizza, south of town by the explosives plant. He'd steal chunks of leftover thermite from the parking lot of the dynamite factory, build rockets out of boosted copper pipe, and send in potato-cam tapes of the launches to cable access. I think he got the last couple models high enough to piss off the FAA, but then he blew off a bunch of fingers trying to light a hot fuse in a demo launch at the K-Mart parking lot by the ghetto mall. They said they could transplant his dick onto his thumb, but he opted for a full amputation and a wooden hand that looked like one of those models you buy at Hobby Lobby for sketching or whatever.

"We're starting a prayer chain for the Jenkins boy," the bottle-blond cashier said, chatting on the corded phone while smacking her gum into the receiver. "Got kicked in the head trying to jerk off a police horse on a meth bender.

Been in a coma for a month now, but they got that Schiavo law, so Medicare can keep 'em on the feeding tubes for years. Jesus up!"

I managed to get down about three bites of pizza, and it gave me food poisoning for days. I lost ten pounds and saved a ton of money on groceries, so at least I had that going for me.

The Kansas City Tofu Firebombing

I'm tired. I'm tired. I'm tired. I swim in the hot and deep waters of a distant consciousness, brief memories of what it was once like to be awake, intercut with the distant vision of life scrolling in front of me, out of my control. It's par for the course. Nobody sleeps in this country anymore; eight hours a night isn't physically possible. A nation exhausted, riding the caffeine/sugar roller coaster to a premature burial. Saying you're sleep-deprived to the point of murder/suicide is as played out as telling someone at the office photocopier you've got a case of the Mondays.

But most people don't let their sleep hygiene get out of control to the point of waking up while driving a car at high speed with a Speak and Spell up their ass and a topographical map of Cedar Point in 1963 carved in their left arm. People generally don't dump cases of Tylenol PM tablets into a meat grinder and mix the pastel blue dust into a box of wine, creating a thick purple paste that can be eaten like cake icing. I've spent more time than could possibly be healthy trying to google up a doctor like that croaker who gave Michael Jackson intravenous anesthesia and rape drugs on a daily basis. And my sleep is bad enough at home. When I'm on the road, all bets are off.

This was a cross-country trip, another cross-country trip, probably the third or fourth time I burned every bridge in life, broke my lease, gave away my furniture, piled the same boxes of nostalgic and useless garbage into a rental car, and drove to the opposite coast to start over. I couldn't even remember if I was going east or west. I started the trip with a bad head cold and a massive Sudafed problem, and at this point, I should have shut the entire thing down, pulled into whatever half-abandoned village scrolled up next on the highway, rented a single-wide trailer, and slept for a month. I wouldn't, though, because I'm an idiot.

I needed food, glucose in my blood stream, something to counteract eating a dessert pizza and a box of donut holes for breakfast and then sugar crashing for hours. I should have packed D5NS IV bags of saline and dextrose to keep me fully topped off for the long trip, but I couldn't find a knockoff handbag store in Chinatown that sold medical supplies before I left, or at least didn't sell bootleg ones that were full of mercury and arsenic. I took the next exit without investigating, followed the food signs, and looked for a hamburger joint or buffet where I could shame-eat five thousand calories and watch enough human failure to feel good about my own life, and maybe stop driving for long enough to think.

A Old Country Shitkicker Buffet on the west edge of town had a salad bar, rare in this part of the country. It consisted of a pan of rotten iceberg lettuce, a few wilted vegetables, and four fully-stocked diabetes-inducing ice cream machines with all the fixins. There was also the usual assortment of greasy meat products and baked goods. I thought I'd load up on croutons and breadsticks before I started the main course, lay a solid base of starch for the USDA Grade-D tri-tip steak food product that cost me an extra $2.99.

A snaggletoothed bleach blonde cut in front of me, filling her tray with salisbury steak chunks and ranch dressing. She wore a halter top, exposing her muffin-top midriff with a tramp stamp that said "daddy's little whore" in faded ink across her stretch-marked skin. I had no interest in an eighteen-year-old girl with four kids and eight abortions, but I also couldn't not look, because I'm a horrible human being.

The skin revealed by her TJ Maxx clearance top was a mixture of spray tan and cellulite. She was at the apex where youth still barely prevailed, and the four daily packs of Marlboro reds hadn't fully amped up the vasoconstriction to destroy her features. The skin tone reminded me of a time my buddy Satanic Duane got the keys to a wax museum a step-cousin of his ran, and invited me to over to fuck the mannequins. It was five lifetimes ago, a classic antics-with-Satanic-Duane time that seemed like a distant dream by now.

* * *

I went with Duane to the museum once, late at night, to check out the dummies. "You gotta see this shit. They have a Rachel Ray that looks like the real thing. No holes, but you

can still use the hands. And the best part is it doesn't talk."
The place was called *Slow Eddie's Famous Figures and Cigs Shop*
and the front door was covered with faded, hand-written
disclaimers stating the shop was in no way related to
Madame Tussaud's or any of the celebrities depicted. The
dolls inside (or statues, or artworks — whatever you call
them) looked like they were stolen from a Taiwanese ware-
house that produced bootleg statues for knockoff wax muse-
ums, and were covered in a thick film of nicotine stains and
grease.

Slow Eddie, the museum owner, ran a smoke shop and
corn dog stand in the back of the gallery. He paid an American Indian guy to come in once a month and get an exemp-
tion for the state's tobacco tax stamps, so his prices were
cheap. He also ran numbers on the weekend, under the table, using a complicated system of coded paper tickets one
would "win" and exchange in the bathroom stall for cash.
But the real attraction was the wax figures, with the blotchy,
yellowing skin, covered in a thin sheen of fryer grease and
stuck-on hair from the rat infestation.

I couldn't fuck a wax figurine in a public museum, especially with the facsimiles of Al Roker, Larry King, and one of
the Star Trek dudes staring at me with their beady glass eyes.
But Duane jumped right in, bending over a doll of Ricardo
Montalbán and screaming quotes about *Fantasy Island* and
rich Corintian leather as he ground away on figurine's ass-
wax. "Smiles, everyone! Smiles! Come on dude, join in —

there's a *Charlie's Angels* exhibit in the back we can run train on, if you're into that. It's the season one cast, too — Farrah and not Diane fucking Ladd."

I didn't do anything with the dolls, and didn't want to watch, so I played with the illegal slot machines until I ran out of money, then got a credit card cash advance and lost another five hundred bucks. Slow Eddie did hook us me with some free corn dogs and cokes, which I shame-ate while I watched my money drizzle away, a quarter at a time.

"Somethin's not right with your friend, is it?" he asked me. "I haven't seen someone fuck Montelbán so much since that back surgeon paralyzed him in the 90s."

"Oh, Duane? He's a Satanist. I mean, he thinks he's a Satanist. I think he read the Wikipedia page once, but never sent in an application or anything."

"Yeah, I'm gonna have to charge him extra. I need to hire an exorcist. We all worship Jesus out here — I can't have any Satanistic jizz on the figurines."

* * *

The bread carb coma wore off, and I found myself in the November cold of a Reno winter at high altitude, my nose bloody, a toilet destroyed, my iPod batteries dead. I was in a cabin in a parking lot next to a 7-Eleven that rented for $17 a night, with no heat, no shower, but unlimited electricity. It also included stolen cable, but no TV. My carb coma dreams were pure sex, bobbling tits in unicorn rainbow shirts and a waterbed fuck that sounded like the Titanic sinking.

A guy pumping gas at the lone Citgo pump in front of the mini-mart banged on the thin plywood door, yelling at me to turn off the porno as I moaned in my sleep. I ignored him, looked for a free Wi-Fi signal on my beaten MacBook, and only found SSIDs connected to local pedophilia sting operations, named "LEGAL TEENS" and "BOY BAND FREE FUCK," 802.11 connections leading straight to a mandatory minimum prison sentence and a daily gang-fuck from every gang in the joint. No thanks.

The mini-mart reminded me of a massive gas station I saw a night, a week, a month ago, in Kansas City. It sat right on the Kansas/Missouri line, so it had a mirror duplicate of itself, two of everything, because of a byzantine gasoline tax law. Dee Snyder worked the left front counter, his makeup gone, always looking like he needed a shower. "I can't sell you beef jerky without a permit. Maybe if you're an American Indian, but I'm gonna need to see some paperwork. And no 'we're not gonna take it' jokes, asshole."

I only needed gas, grass, ass. A night on the couch of an old reform school buddy left a permanent dent in my spine, right between the sixth and seventh vertebrae. They sell a kit online to fix that yourself, but you need a plunge router and a lot of gauze. And make goddamn sure you hold that spinning bit at exactly ninety degrees when you jam it into your back, because you don't want that shit to go sideways and leave you confined to a bed for the rest of your life, paying an illegal immigrant "massage therapist" to jam a piece of pipe in your ass every day so you can take a shit Chris Reeve style into a bag.

I needed reading material to keep my mind off of things, but could only find a rack of Harley mags and farmer porn, plus a giant pictorial on Jesus. Pictures of Jesus. A magazine of pictures on Jesus. I guess that's a one-shot — you're not going to have much sequel potential there if they hung him up at 33.

That was Kansas. My school buddy Seth, was a vegan, and insisted we firebomb the very beef and pork places I wanted to devour. "It's all in the sauce, anyway. I know a place that slow-roasts tofu, it's just as good." I didn't believe him, but couldn't afford a hotel. The tofu tasted like hot garbage, and the fermented bean curd nonsense made me shit my pants for the whole drive to St. Louis, and all the way into Terre Haute.

* * *

I waited for an egg plate and a side of death while the waitress rambled her hippy mantra. The drive became so confusing, so monotonous, I could only remember the meals and the bowel movements, but never the sequence in which they happened. The lunch counter was in the bottom floor of a department store, a main-drag all-in-one that sold janitorial work clothes, dynamite, rat poison, shotgun shells, and groceries. People in hunting gear would drive their pickups into town and shop for dog food and fishing gear, then catch a cup of coffee with Edna and ask about her canned goods. I thought about buying a ball jar full of her signature pickled green beans, but a strong case of botulism is a bitch.

"X-Acto futures and the love of god will overcome us all." She stabbed herself in the thigh with a butter knife, and looked at me with the gaze of a grainy-filmed before picture of an exorcism. I expected someone to bust through a wall and yell "HI I'M JOHNNY KNOXVILLE AND THIS IS JACKASS" and play the Minutemen song "Corona" but it never happened. My eggs were cold, too.

Bugs crawled on my skin, invisible bugs, maybe a contact dermatitis. The sound-canceling headphones would never mute out the screams of torture from a bad dozen-hour flight with three connections and no food, and the batteries died anyway. I considered throwing them out the window of the car earlier, but an ominous, unremovable sticker on the cord said something something toxic electronic waste in the state of California, something something $50,000 fine, and I knew I'd be the first person successfully charged on that one, like that asshole who went to pound-you-in-the-ass prison for downloading a Creed album.

"You shouldn't make rape jokes about prison. A lot of prison gangs don't use forced anal sex as a domination tactic anymore. Now that they can get Facebook in there, it's all about trolling and cyber-bullying." The guy pumping my gas at the two-pump station looked like Larry Bird's cousin who could never pass the GED. I didn't think this state — Colorado or Nevada or Nebraska or some other square state — had the New Jersey/Oregon law where an attendant had to pump your fuel, but the guy offered without asking. "Pruno-shaming is a bigger problem than you'd think. Nothing worse than the peer pressure of a group of inmates telling you that you're using too much ketchup in your home-brewed toilet hooch.

"Consensual butt stuff is fine though, if you're into that. Just did a two-year stretch in the Florence Supermax. Nothing violent or sexy though. The fuckin' judge gave me a bullshit charge for aggravated couch fucking after I cleaned out my maw maw's pension and spent it on weed and tacos."

The pump clicked full, and he started jumping up and down on the back bumper, trying to get another tenth of a gallon in there. I saw the pump had a state Weights and Measures sticker from 1987 that said the fuel was 29 octane, certain to ping and knock my engine to its death. "You can't let prison define you, though. It's hard living out here on the mesa — we don't even have HBO. You checked out that show *Girls* yet? I heard that chick's a feminist. I'm into that, I think. Hairy chicks! I'll fuck anything that moves, haha!"

I went inside the one-room store and looked for a fuel additive with octane or lead or whatever it is that turns cheap unleaded gas into pure jet fuel. I had a friend

Groovin' Gary back in high school who was majorly into drag racing, and told me about it, fuel additive salvation.

Groovin' Gary put a 454 Chevy big block into an AMC Gremlin, a pair of foot-wide slicks in the back, and a set of tiny donut spares on the front wheels. He found a chain steering wheel at a yard sale for five bucks, but didn't have the dough for the full-on funny car body, so he cut the rear wheel wells out with an axe. "Weight savings," Gary said. "And proper tools are for rich losers. Duct tape meme, lol." You could watch the super-wide tires rotate through the giant holes in the floor where the back seat used to be. It added to the illusion of speed, or maybe it was the exhaust fumes.

The car would take him twenty minutes to start in cool weather, the engine completely hillbillied into the new vehicle, the donor not even the same make and model. All the emissions gear was long gone; the connections between car and powerplant were tenuous at best, twist-ties and duct tape keeping throttle cables and ignition wires in place. He'd repeat the same ritual after school every day: hood open, shooting starter fluid into the carb, fucking with a manual choke, jamming a screwdriver into the air intake, cranking the engine for five, ten minutes straight.

Gary was into drag racing, the quarter-mile out at the old Osceola speedway, but he also dressed in drag for the races, and sometimes at school. "I like to get the shit beat out of me by the football team. Lets me know I'm alive.

Someday those fuckers will lose their hair and get fat and sell gas grills for a living, and I'll be out in Bakersfield, doing wheelie stands in a Top Fuel car. I don't give a fuck. It's all punk rock to me."

When he'd get the engine running, no exhaust at all, the thunder of seven liters of pure gas-chugging power, we'd find an empty wing of a mall parking lot, pour down some bleach on the pavement, and burn some donuts, the acrid blue smoke filling the interior of the car like a Nazi death chamber through those no-wheel-well floorboards. "Kobe!" Gary screamed for no reason, twisting the chain steering wheel, throwing us around the inside of the Gremlin, nothing but a mash-up of RuPaul wigs, Sabbath blasting in the tape deck, and cheap slicks getting burned into nothing, until a mall cop waddled over, no Segways back in the day, and started yelling about sending us to juvie. Quick exit, we'd hit the county roads, let the smoke smell dissipate, and fire one up for Iommi, our master.

I couldn't find the same fuel additive as Gary's favorite brand from back in the day — some CARB regulation, nationwide ban, birth defects in unborn children, whatever pussy excuse they used to take it off the shelf. "They will tell you how to quit drinking leaded gasoline. You will not listen. The freaks will tell you about EPA studies and California Air Resources Board analysis, but everyone knows a little bit of lead is good for you. Puts hair on your balls." A quick google check told me a can of Chuck Norris energy drink would do the job. I got two from the bizarro hick from French Lick, one for me, one for the car. I had no idea how many miles, days, weeks until my destination. Maybe the journey was the destination. Maybe I was already dead.

Corpses In Wind-shield Are Closer Than They Appear

"Udder Budder, the natural lubricant. Don't forget the double D for discount. Ask for us by name at the hammer section of your local J.L. Perry store. Proudly made in the US of A by honest, hard-working men of superior breeding stock. Our manufacturing plant is made from 100% peanut products. All lives matter. Allergies are a lie!"

Throw the RC Cola bottle at the color TV to turn it off, keep the cap for bonus points. I collected the bottle tops to win the Bell Aerosystems Rocket Belt advertised in the commercials for ten million Loyal Royal Points, peeling back the cork liners from each metal cap to see if I won the grand prize of a free trip to Cott Beverage Land and first crack at the new roller coaster, The Stigmata Twister. (It was a religious theme park. They bought a Demon Drop and repainted it to be about Jesus.)

I stripped my fingers into bloody nubs, bamboo-under-fingernail torture, and could barely read the cap inside. TRY AGAIN. TRY AGAIN. TRY AGAIN. Jimmy Tajara at school got a game piece for a free six-pack of Jesus Juice Cola, but he drowned in a swimming pool a week later, and nobody could find the winning bottle cap. Some kids thought he was buried with it and dug up his grave a month later, but his parents cremated the body (some religious thing, or maybe a fear of zombies) and buried the ashes. The mortician put pieces of a dismembered dead hooker in the kid-sized coffin, along with a hundred copies of the Atari 2600 ET cartridge, for weight. No sign of the bottle cap.

I remember it happening like yesterday: the unholy mixture of air-raid sirens and MC Hammer karaoke music, the interrupted internet, a cacophony of messages: we have found Atlantis; we raised the Titanic; the ISS Space Station has fallen out of orbit; Coke Classic will be discontinued. Crystal Pepsi is back. If you fear change, prepare for the ultimate in butt-hurt. The headlines echoed like that "We Didn't Start the Fire" song, and I prayed a Soviet EMP weapon would soon explode over our heads and take out every cassette tape Soundesign karaoke machine for five thousand miles.

This was the year I broke my right arm in a freak lobster accident — tried attaching a nutcracker for the claws on an old timey merry-go-round, then sending the lobsters back in time through a DeLorean machine so I'd see them as a kid, try to warn myself of how I'd grow up. Butter everywhere, I slipped and fell, the kid broke his arm at the same time — I think Rod Serling ripped off the idea for a TV show once. Had to jerk off with my left hand for six months — cross-training — have I told this story already? I can't remember anything anymore. Tried using pumice powder made out of aluminum and asbestos to scrub my teeth clean while my good brushing arm was tied up in the sling. Brushing with your wrong hand is harder than you'd think. Got them white as a golf resort on Easter, but I think it ate away the top level of enamel. My teeth are green stumps now, look like a bunch of swamp creatures standing in a row. I don't care, I'll buy a boat and people will love me.

A road crew of DUI work-release inmates sprayed tanning solution on the zoo animals from a fire department pump truck. The dinosaur cloning place sent the safari park a batch of velociraptors with the albino gene set at the breeding factory, and the bright white ancient reptiles didn't look scary enough to justify the $34.95 admission price. (Seniors only $29.95 before 4:00 on Tuesdays. Veterans two for one — we support the troops!) The work crew accidentally used a spray tan chemical with an estrogen supplement, popular with all the Instagram stars and Hollywood wannabes — and the dinosaurs all grew massive tits. Oh well, thought the flunkie park manager. Raise the ticket price a few more bucks, call it Velociraptors After Dark. Hope Cinemax and Spielberg won't sue.

I think I'm allergic to horses, but I've never seen one. My parents used to burn old furniture in our living room for heat — something about protesting OPEC back in the Carter years. All the smoldering horse glue must have got into my lungs, caused a sensitivity. My folks thought I was allergic to chocolate, used to beat me senseless every Halloween, Easter, Christmas. Pretty much every holiday as a kid involved chocolate, at least the fake stuff they called chocolate in America back then. I know chocolate snobs look at that Hershey shit like asshole craft homebrew enthusiasts treat Miller Lite. But my folks lost their shit anyway. Even chocolate milk — how much actual chocolate is in that, anyway? They probably put two teaspoons of weak-ass Nestle Quik per tanker truck of the stuff, but that was enough to make my parents load me up on Benadryl until I was unconscious for a month any time the cafeteria workers gave me a little half-pint cardboard carton of the stuff.

* * *

She didn't even hear the jogger's body hit the grill of the truck. Kept on driving with a corpse sticking out of her windshield, arms and legs flailing in the air, the severed jugular spraying blood into the cockpit. Drove another 18 miles like that, pulled into a HyVee and went inside and did her weekly grocery shopping. Came back out, twenty minutes later, six bags of groceries and a couple of cases of soda pop, loaded it all in the hatchback, the body still stuck in the front windscreen.

The pedestrian was still alive — the Rain-X spray on the window worked as a coagulant, sealed shut the spurting neck wounds. But once she got the truck back up to highway speeds on the toll road, she hit a deer, same side of the car, and the antlers impaled the guy, total fatality. The cops found the mess, intertwined corpses and blood, in the woman's carport the next day. They weren't sure if they were serial collisions, or if a guy was trying to fuck a deer and got hit by a car. They don't have rape kits for deer, and if they did, the state would make the deer pay for it. The deer was asking for it. Maybe it shouldn't have dressed like a deer slut.

"Took us two days to clean up the shit from that carport. Deer crap everywhere — and that stuff will give you the lime disease, whatever the fuck it's called, deer AIDS. That chick from *The Real World* caught it, the one that got slapped in the face. I think she died from it, or maybe pop rocks and Diet Coke. And you can't just scrape off deer scat — it's not all solid pellets, if they've been eating softer foods. You've gotta steam it out, then load up a power washer with TSP, cut with bleach. That pulls the paint right off metal, too. You could probably strip a skeleton bare with that stuff, straight down to bleach-white bones."

The cleaning guy who stripped and sprayed my vomit-filled motel bed knew about the bleach trick, because he *had* stripped skeletons bare in the crawl space of his house. Every Thursday, drunk on as much Everclear and gas station wine as he could buy with his paycheck, he'd cruise the college gay bars for prey, bring them back to his house to watch the WCW Thunder broadcast. He'd coax the twink kids he picked up into doing some wrestling moves, slow and sexy-like. He'd show them his best Mike Awesome Chokebomb, then hit them with a rag of chloroform.

He'd watch the rest of the WCW broadcast with the corpse, have sex with the dead body a few more times, cook a huge dinner of French food, and then later strip the flesh from the dead body and write in his manifesto about how he was compelled to kill because of habitually watching *Brady Bunch* episodes on PCP as a young teen After his murder trial, they would demolish his entire apartment building, then build a Walgreen's drug store there.

During the dedication of the store, a local child actor dressed as Fredo Corleone would impregnate a Las Vegas prostitute. Then his brother would row him out into Lake Michigan in a fishing boat and shot him in the head, for disgracing their family. The whole thing was captured on a multimedia interactive DVD-ROM, but nobody really got into it because it used the Java browser plugin player, and fuck Java.

* * *

The news showed a man with a walrus mustache and a "love it or leave it" hat telling the reporter why it was every white male's god-given right to carry an FIM-92 Stinger missile to a psych hospital. In the background of the live shot, two fat kids with bowl haircuts flashed gang symbols, while the men's rights activist tried to explain his open carry philosophy. "In *Terminator 2*, that cyborg came in with a loaded shotgun in a box of flowers and started blowing people away. I've got two nephews and an old pastor locked up here for psychosexual crimes they probably didn't commit, and when I'm visiting, I want to keep my family and fellow patriots safe. An armed society is a polite society, you piece of shit. Go fuck your mother."

Two freaky East German dudes in the car dealership went from vehicle to vehicle, sniffing the leather seats of every Toyota on the lot. They looked like the kind of guys who listened to too much Kraftwerk and watched videos of women with excessive facial hair shitting on expensive synthesizers while writing academic papers about aesthetics. I laid low in the service lounge, ignoring the blaring TV, searching for elephantiasis articles, trying to find meaning in life via laptop surfing on slow Wi-Fi while they overcharged me for a brake job I didn't need. Cars never really need service anymore, unless you royally fuck them up. You can drive the average econobox for 500,000 miles without doing much except adding gas and keeping air in the tires.

A woman sat across from me in the lounge, a solid 7/10, but herding four kids by five dads, rocking a set of Daffy Duck sweats that screamed "I've given up on life, ask me about my grandkids in ten years." She was changing a diaper on top of a microwave oven in the customer lounge while the other three kids smashed out windows with a tire iron they stole from the parts department. I tried not to acknowledge her, kept at my computer, and frantically did everything possible to not imagine her without kids but with the same amount of self-deprecation, and actually interested in failed writers racking up unnecessary repairs on their cars.

I had this new bullshit mindfulness meditation practice that I got from a YouTube video I found while surfing for nude yoga documentaries. You're supposed to gaze at a picture of a farmhouse from 19th-century Russia and imagine all the people who died there of starvation and dysentery to push everything else out of your mind. The more I stared at this black and white JPEG in my web browser, the more I thought about how I should sell everything I own, buy a one-way plane ticket to Vladivostok, and start walking north until I died of exposure. It's either that or buy a Corvette, but license plates and insurance are so goddamn expensive, especially with that gas guzzler tax. Also those new Corvettes look like straight-up carbon-fiber bullshit. What was Chevy thinking with that new C7 design? Is there a sequel to the *Transformers* movie coming up I don't know about? Ugh.

I went to google to check the cost of plane tickets to Siberia in one tab and open the Chevy build-a-car site in another, but my laptop was infested with pop-up ads for vintage pre-WW1 enema gloves, apparently from some thing I fell into while knocked out on Ambien the night before. I would need to uninstall and reinstall my browser five times and try not to kill anyone, which would be impossible. If I was a kid, I would steal a crowbar and start breaking headlights, but I knew I'd get caught and thrown into pound-you-in-the-ass federal prison on trumped-up terrorism charges.

After a series of divorces and marriages, the single mom would bag a rich guy with some kind of millionaire cattle ranching business, and the oldest kid would go nuts, kill five people, and get caught shoving an entire case of beer up his ass at an AM/PM gas station mart. He'd plead affluenza in the criminal case, and during discovery, the prosecution would discover the mom had the largest collection of beanie babies ever found in the state of Texas. He'd get 30 days of picking up trash for the crimes, but hire some Mexicans from a Home Depot parking lot to do it for him while he played *Excitebike* on a vintage Nintendo all day.

Jesus Ray Liotta and the Laxative Recall Boondoggle

Johnny Monoxide knew no fear. He ate three Lunchables and was Ready to Fuck. He carved a drawing of the Haunted Mansion (from LA, not the bullshit one in Orlando) into his thigh with a dull hobby knife, and slapped a slice of Oscar Meyer ham and swiss loaf on the bleeding wound to keep it cheesy. Everyone in the parking lot of the Dollar General knew he meant Real Business. He vaped kaopetate and salsa, waiting for his mom to pick him up after her fiber arts meet-up.

"Did you see that kid with the hobby knife? He looked like a Jewish Burt Lancaster." The two construction workers carried metal lunch pails filled with raw organ meats in baby food jars, the latest diet fad for the cheap and stupid. They wanted to find a predatory victim for a threesome-slash-murder, but ended up at a Gamestop, trying out the virtual reality version of BattleToads. (Call them and ask about it.)

"I know his dad, I think. He's got an IMDB page. He was jerking off at a taping of *Punky Brewster* and because of some union disagreement, Brandon Tartikoff gave him an executive producer credit. The discussion page is used by

ISIL operatives to coordinate terror strikes. He used to eat at the 'cheese back when I still busted heads over there." Before getting into construction, the worker managed a Chuck-E-Cheese, until all the mom-bod tits drove him nuts. That led to a brief career in dentistry, then local politics, then construction. In six months, he'd either be an Uber driver or a surgeon. It could go either way. Disruption economy meme.

The first man had an epiphany, a sudden vision of Christ on a long pier at Coney Island, looking at a light-house, eating a Nathan's hot dog and dripping brown mustard on his shroud. The Jesus figure looked like a Ray Liotta version of Jesus — not a *Goodfellas* Ray Liotta, but more like a *Muppets Most Wanted* Ray Liotta. His stigmata were incorrectly located in his hands (they need to be in the wrists to hold the weight of the body — try it yourself) and the crown of thorns was made of Helical brand stainless steel razor wire. The Liotta Christ chewed with his mouth open and told the man about Plumpy Nut, a peanut-based paste produced by the French company Nutriset and distributed in 92-gram plastic packs to third-world countries as a Ready-to-Use Therapeutic Food (RUTF). In the United States, peanut products are all but banned, perceived as dangerous as land mines or Agent Orange. But in rural Somalia, the stuff was dropped out of airplanes and bigger than Jesus, Ray Liotta or otherwise.

The man fell to the ground in a seizure after seeing the apparition. The kid's mom showed up and drove him home.

His Haunted Mansion scarification left his jorts completely drenched in blood, but his mom had plenty of Liquid Tide to bust that shit up. (The dad wasn't home — he was out sucking a dentist's dick for Tide money.)

* * *

I watched a TV show called *Thinkin' Bout Dick*, a mid-season replacement starring some female rapper I did not know, and Mike Tyson in drag. The TV was mounted from the ceiling of the genetics lab in a bulletproof plastic box, aged yellow with nicotine and piss. I was there to get tested to see if I had that condition where cilantro tastes like soap. I knew that was the case, but for some reason, I wanted the genetic test done anyway.

I couldn't change the channel, didn't bring a book, and needed to ignore the other guy in the waiting room, who kept mumbling "Madagascar. NASCAR. Madagascar. NASCAR." He was a beat-down detective from the internet crime division, and fucked around with an AOL floppy disk, trying to pry loose the metal shutter for use as a circumcision device. "Shit ain't gonna work. You know how long these tests take?"

A technician behind a red curtain operated a blood spinner device. He dressed as the Wizard of Oz, and sequenced DNA while playing *Lemmings* on an old-school Nintendo GameBoy. "Mhmm, DNA. Hmhmm." Dr. Cwm was renowned for his upper gastrointestinal work, and for being the only Harvard-educated surgeon to have no vowels in his name. But after the lawsuit, he lost his surgery privileges, had to resort to running the dodgy genetics lab to make bank.

Cwm mumbled into a McDonald's headset hooked to a transcription tape recorder, an experiment in creating audio books to sell online. He needed the money for a lung transplant. Well, *needed* was a strong word; he seriously *wanted* a lung transplant, because he liked the look of the scars. He found a guy on Craigslist who would cut open his skin to get the right look, but he wanted the full deal.

"I am sick of waiting on this shit," said the detective guy. "I think he's just fucking with us. I want to go to Target and buy every Pizza Hut Personal Pan they have baking under the lights there. I don't care when the best-by date is — those are bullshit anyway, those pizzas will last ten years under ideal temperatures. I would blow five guys nine times for some breadsticks. And yes, math-impaired readers, that means I would suck a total of 45 dicks for those breadsticks. And fuck common core math — I will show my work the old way."

I could not stand the tinkertoy abortion roadside attraction level of professionalism anymore. I yelled at the fake doctor to cancel my test and give me a medical marijuana license as a consolation prize. I wasted enough time that day; the least they could do is validate my parking and give me some free Narcan tablets, do-it-yourself IUD kits, or boner stay-hard topical ointment.

He scribbled on a prescription pad in magic marker. "Give this to your insurance, and if they don't take it, fuck the police. And come see my harsh noise band Cym Zyzzyva at the Knitting Factory next Tuesday. I play the theremin and sledgehammer. Capri Sun forever, and peace out, bitches." The doctor yelled "GOGOGO" and a trap door opened under his desk, vanishing him into the floor before I could ask him about the penis cream situation.

The insurance slip said I could vanish without a trace and spend sixteen weeks in a German spa under an assumed name, all spelled out in doctor-speak, with various diagnosis and billing codes that looked legit enough to me. If that didn't work, I'd vanish into the jungles of Cambodia, and build an underground tunnel system with pieces of crashed military jets, until my supply of Power Bars ran out and I had to eat the local food. (I don't deal with Cambodian food that well — I found this out at that *Apocalypse Now*-themed restaurant in Vegas.)

Back in the waiting room, a receptionist who looked like a chubby Tonya Harding wrote me an appointment reminder in crayon, asking me something about my favorite Drake's Cake and if I ever showed my dick to a leprechaun. It may have been St. Patrick's day — I never pay attention to ethnic pride holidays, since I can't exploit them for benefit, and I don't drink green beer. I folded up the appointment card, and ignored her insurance referrals for peak lung volume and galvanic skin response studies. I didn't need any more unnecessary medical tests, at least not that week.

I walked down a long hospital tunnel of white walls and ceiling, like the gantry crane to a Space Shuttle to Mars that was never built. The maze of torment inside the hospital building made me feel like a seizure was coming up. I ended up in a 10th-century mall of sausage factories and outdated calculator repair shops, the kind of place budget Christian plus-size work clothing stores go to die.

After 45 minutes of walking down the corridor, a guy appeared, with Einstein hair, the mottled skin of an 18th-century seafarer, and a vape pen shaped like a dog's dick. "Hey man, you wanna buy a UFO?" His vape dong spewed smoke that smelled of Christmas spices and car battery innards. "Five bucks. I can't show it to you first, but it's got all features."

"What do you mean 'all features?' Like, it has a face?"

"Eyes without a face, lol. No, I mean bluetooth, AM/FM, air conditioning, whitewalls. It's 1:72 scale but it's in the seventh dimension, so that's really like 504 feet."

I closed my eyes and tried to focus on a distant memory of being in Benton Harbor, Michigan, buying a gallon of distilled water to mix with pool chemicals and Listerine as a birth control method. It's illegal to buy bottled water in Berrien County on a Sunday — some obscure blue law — and I drove to Canada instead. While I was there, at some department store like a Sears — maybe Hudson's Bay, but it seemed too run down and fucked to be a 'Bay — I bought a Rush tape and realized that all Canadian cassettes had black plastic shells instead of the usual beige-white of American releases. I never figured out why, and trying to google an answer just brought me to a thousand results of Black Sabbath albums on tape, so who knows. Someone tell me if you know. Or maybe I imagined this.

I opened my eyes, and the UFO guy was gone. The hallway smelled sterile, like they spent a thousand dollars a minute air conditioning it, like the machine rooms where they hold Cray mainframe computers. Outside, it smelled like crack cocaine secondhand smoke and rotting garbage, so I considered spending all day in the hallway. But within four minutes, I got bored, and went to a MusicLand to make fun of the Men Without Hats albums, until the fake restaurants nearby opened for lunch.

* * *

The taco pornography place must have been authentic, because an entire quinceañera party ate chimichangas and monster burritos in the narrow shotgun galley restaurant like starved hyenas set loose in a hamburger factory, dripping hot salsa and grease all over their cheap rental tuxedos and neon fuchsia low-cut dresses. A sign behind the self-serve cash register said "no refunds in the event of death" and I wondered what chain of misfortune ended up causing that one. Every legal disclaimer involved some ridiculous lawsuit. No Shoes,

No Shirt, No Service must have resulted from one hell of a bad day to get stuck with jury duty. Still, they had five tacos for a dollar, so I couldn't complain.

The restaurant only had a few loose tables and a narrow bar against one wall, actually just a piece of lumber nailed lengthwise where you could balance a single taco and a nudie mag to eat and jerk. I sat at a two-top that hadn't been cleaned since the Korean War, and got into it with a taco plate, extra cheese, and a dumpy housewife confessions mag from the early 80s. It only had four pages of color pics, the rest dumb, grammatically incorrect stories printed on news pulp that looked like rough institutional paper towels.

A second later, a woman sat next to me. She had a narrow waist, breeder hips, but the face of the Crypt Keeper, and stringy hair to match. She was down to fuck, but wore a *Designing Women* pantsuit, and it wasn't 1986 anymore, so no. I focused on my food, and hoped she didn't run a destitution scheme on me, or pull out her flip-phone and start talking to her great-great-grandchildren while I was trying to eat.

Ten minutes into tacos and chill, I realized I accidentally gave the robot pornographer a debit card, and they seized my entire checking account balance as a deposit on the silverware and plastic tray, throwing my financial existence in limbo. I called the bank's 800 number for support, and expected the worst. "It's just a temporary hold," the Syrian child labor agent on the phone told me. "You'll get back your funds within a month. A year, tops."

The cashier also ran an intricate long con when people weren't paying attention. I watched him do it five times — it involved adding a five-cent bottle deposit onto the sale of each taco, then pocketing the money at the end of each night. Nobody looks at the receipt for a taco. I think that was a Mitch Hedberg joke, wasn't it? Or was it donuts?

"I wrote a book about zombies and enemas." They guy behind the counter wouldn't shut up, and I was stuck listening because there were no more napkins, and only one guy was working the kitchen, and when I asked him to go in the back and get me a napkin, he started crying and telling me about his entire life, starting with how his mom wouldn't buy him a *Six Million Dollar Man* doll in 1976. "I used to take those phospo-soda laxatives all the time, the kind that they give you before a colon-camera roto-rooter, you know? Made me like a Mr. Coffee — pour cold water in the top, and a second later, hot water shoots out the bottom. But they started banning those things a few years ago."

"Why, are they addictive?" I imagined a black market for laxative junkies, trading stolen jewelry and car stereos for little half-melted bars of Ex-Lax and hippie herbal tea that makes you shit. Low-end hookers leaning on your car windows outside the Holland Tunnel, offering to suck your dick for a jug of Metamucil. MiraLAX speakeasies. Milk of Magnesia bordellos. Senokot dens.

Vol. 13

"No, product recall. Something about it makes your kidneys go out? It screws up your electrolytes. Just drink some Gatorade, right? So now I gotta take The Nozzle. Grease it up, jam it in — the deluge. The Big Squirt. We're talking enemas, bro. Speaking of, you getting extra guacamole on your tacos?"

The no-Steve-Austin-doll guy behind the counter pulled a cloned meat slab from the freezer, and cut it into strips using a custom-made patented food extrusion blade, a proprietary tool designed by the franchised food giant to more efficiently divide and process the assholes and eyeballs for maximum profitability. I suddenly recognized the guy, from a YouTube video where some skate punks built Viking weapons out of wooden pallets and beat each other senseless while shouting Black Flag lyrics they didn't understand. (There was one video where they were singing "TB party tonight! TB party tonight!" and giving each other tuberculosis.) At least I think it was the same kid — I sometimes wonder if I have that disease where you can't recognize faces. I also wish I could remember the name of that disease, so I could tell future employers I had it.

"Seriously, that chick in the Weight Watchers ad is so hot, I would kill every one of my childhood pets five times just to hear her fart through a Speak and Spell. If she was the head of a human centipede and I was the tail segment, I'd still pay extra." I had no idea what or who he was talking about. "Hey man, text me your digits, and I'll tell you next time we have guacamole on sale." I reluctantly did, and he sent me a barrage of messages over the next month, mostly about how his neighbor's dog was telling him to shoot people, or something horribly stereotypical.

Outside, a group of hobos lit cars on fire for warmth, like a *Mad Max* movie with a smaller budget. One of the men wore severed arms as mittens, and swung around a staff weapon crafted from the femurs of innocent bystanders. I sometimes wonder why these people wouldn't use a fraction of the ingenuity and effort required to build a shanty town out of discarded tampons and stolen building supplies and, you know, travel to Mars and back, run successful Fortune 500 companies, something. But I'm sure it's a complicated problem. I can't even win at *Sim City*, so how the hell am I supposed to know the answers to life anyway? I didn't even know the answer to how I was going to get through my god damned taco plate without puking.

* * *

His last text to me was "LOL" before he crashed his brother's plane into a Holiday Inn. I thought about sending a screencap to CafePress or Shutterfly and making a coffee mug or throw pillow with the image burned on it for all of eternity, but I decided to wait until I found a 50% off promo code. Plenty of time between now and forever, especially when it involves saving seventeen dollars.

"He left this life like he lived it: in extreme stupidity," I told the woman standing next to me at the Wimpy Burger.

"Wha? You calling me stupid?"

"No, the plane wreck guy." I pointed to a news monitor on the wall, but it already flickered to the next story in the cycle, about a man who lost weight by filling every bathtub in his house with piss. I don't know the science behind it, just that you needed at least four tubs to get it to work, and I've only got a small efficiency bath with a stand-up shower, so it didn't look like I had any weight loss in my immediate future.

"YJJJUUOOOO — LIGHTTHT UPPPHH MAAAAII-IHH LIGGGHFFFF!" A morbidly obsese man in Lakers jersey, either a crackhead or a stroke victim (or maybe both), cut in line in front of everyone, singing the Debby Boone love song to the cashier. The woman behind the register ignored him, playing one of those jewel-tap games on an off-brand prepaid cell phone that blared a Rihanna song through its tiny speaker. A fry cook behind her ignored five baskets of burning fries billowing dank black smoke through the restaurant. He read from a photocopy of the original D&D *Monster Manual*, wondering if centaurs had one dong or two.

Normally, I'd be borderline homicidal with the lack of customer service, but I was still perplexed by the plane crash. How do you wreck a Cessna, anyway? You basically can't even stall one of those fucking things; pull the stick all the way back, and it just sort of laughs at you, droops the wings for a second, and takes off again. It's like trying to kill yourself in a Yugo — you can drive it at full speed into a brick wall and not even scratch the bumper. He must have had a strong anti-life gene in his brain, a DNA-encoded death wish. I'd heard of people killing themselves with a butter knife. Or maybe that was in an Adam Sandler movie. It all blurs together now.

"I hope this bitch puts down her phone soon. I've gotta take a dump, and I need more fries." The woman in front of me wore a mu mu and smelled of death and plague, like the zombie vial of fluid concentrate in a Smell-O-Vision movie from the Sixties. I wondered if a diet of nothing but fast food caused the smell, like her pores oozed trans-fats, or if the sickness or genetic disorder troubling her caused an unending craving for bad food — what's the cart, what's the horse. Either way, I hoped it was not contagious. Earlier in the week, there was news about how airborne AIDS designed by the US Navy was suddenly coming into vogue as a club drug, and we'd all be doomed. I guess it could be worse — I could be working as a fry cook, too poor to buy a real hardcopy of the *Monster Manual*.

"YOUUUGUG GIIFFFF MEE HOOOPPHHHG TOOOO CARRREEYEEY ONNNNN" I was going to give the guy two more verses, before I called 911 and reported an active Muslim shooter so I could get my goddamn lunch.

The Open Letter to S.C. Johnson & Son, A Family Company

Dear S. C. Johnson & Son, Inc:

I am writing to complain about the overtly sexual connotations of your Scrubbing Bubbles product. I typically drink two or three cans of Scrubbing Bubbles a day while performing abortions at a local Checker gas station, and like to listen to old 78 records of pornographic negro spirituals, the nasty stuff you can't even buy mail-order anymore, the kind of albums collected by white supremacists who can only get off while being fucked in the ass while listening to them. And while I drank my Scrubbing Bubbles the other day, mixed 50/50 with Dexron transmission fluid and a dash of bitters, a man dressed as the Burger Chef mascot approached me and asked, "Do you know anything about the legend of The Tocopherol Road Monster?" I had not, and he spent the next 45 minutes explaining it to me.

Couples used to "neck" on Tocopherol Road, south of town, past the covert landing strip where the Senate Judiciary Committee flew in bales of methamphetamine precursors during the Clinton presidency, back when a consortium of drug kingpins, Federal judges, and home improvement show hosts used AOL chat to organize murder-for-hire rings with drug-crazed prostitutes cross-dressed as cast members of *The Jeffersons*. I didn't know what "neck" meant, but I looked it up on Urban Dictionary, and it either means when you kiss someone without any further sexual relations, or when you cut off their head and fuck their throat tubes. Anyway, the couples would go and "neck" (the old, not-fun way not involving esophageal intercourse) and this one time the guy got out of the car to take a dump, probably from eating ten chili dogs at an A&W drive-in, and he told the girl to not move or unlock the door, and not think or learn to read or get a bank account or ever take a job or become a productive member of society, and she agreed, because this was like 287 years ago, and it's a fucked up little backwater town that tried to ban fluorescent lights once because they're not in the Old Testament and someone started a rumor that the gays were trying to shove them up their asses, which then caused a bunch of people to try shoving them up their asses, causing a rash of ER cases of dudes with broken poisonous glass fragments embedded in their assholes.

The guy goes to take a shit, and the woman sits there listening to the AM radio for a long time, and he never comes back. And then there's this scraping noise on the roof of the car, and she thinks it's the branches of the trees above, swaying in the wind. Then there's a tapping on the car window, and she's scared, but it turns out it's a cop, and he tells her she has to leave and he'll take her home, but not to look back at the car. And he leads her back to the cop car, and she turns, and the dude is hanging from a tree, all dismembered with his junk cut out and his blood sprayed everywhere, and his dangling arms are scraping on the roof of the car. And that's the legend of the Tocopherol Road Monster.

And right after the guy explains it to me, I ask him what kind of car the dude drove, because one time I had a chance to buy a '67 Nova SS 396, which is really rare, but some idiot had taken out the 396 and replaced it with a cheap 307 small-block, but I still figured it would be worth buying and restoring, and then some other prick outbid me, and a week later wrapped it around a tree, and I've always wondered about old cars and if coincidentally that dead dude's car was the same SS 396. And there's always these urban legends of guys seeing a Corvette for $500 in the newspaper, and it turns out some dude got shot in it and his body sat there for a year, and the inside of the car smelled like a Taco Bell bathroom, and I figured if the guy's going to tell me one urban legend, maybe he can string together a few, and close with the Jamaican Toothbrush Bandit or maybe Mikey from Life Cereal getting his jizz-filled stomach pumped at a Rod Stewart concert.

The guy in the Burger Chef suit got all pissed off and left, drove his car to a secret military installation in New

Mexico, where the government would later pay RAND a large amount of money to hire a bunch of philosophy majors and stoners and science-fiction writers and linguists to come up with a way to tell future civilizations not to dig ten thousand feet into the earth and turn this nuclear waste dump into a drinking well for little kids, and one of the people on this committee was Keith Emerson from the band Emerson Lake and Palmer, and he was all butt-hurt about Lester Bangs slagging him in a review (I think in *Creem* magazine, it was later reprinted in one of his books, that *Carburetor Dung* one, I think) and he went on and on about how fucked analog synthesizers were, and how he had this one old Taurus synth that took up four rooms of his London flat, and would actually take about twelve days to fully power up, and he could set all of the dials and knobs to make a certain sound, then go to eat lunch at a shitty macrobiotic lunch place out in Marble Arch and come back two hours later, having not touched a single goddamn thing, and the sound would be completely different.

And while he wasted an entire afternoon of everyone's time, a nuclear physicist came up with the idea to start a Manhattan Project-level effort to clone human beings, and then they would continually clone Keith Emerson, let each clone live for a few hours, and then violently kill him, but interleave the clones in such a way that a clone would always be living at the New Mexico facility (about 25 miles north-northwest of the Carlsbad Caverns) and then in 10,000 years, when future civilizations or aliens or whatever else came and thought about drilling into the nuclear waste facility, there would be a Keith Emerson clone, talking about what a raw deal his band 3 got (a brief power-pop trio consisting of Emerson, Carl Palmer, and Robert Berry, that produced one horrible album, *To the Power of Three*, in 1988. Berry is best known for replacing Steve Hackett in an aborted attempt at reforming the band GTR. The album had almost none of the signature sound of ELP and was written to be incredibly radio-friendly, and was largely a critical failure. The band actually toured as Emerson and Palmer, probably because 3 is a stupid name for a band, except now that album always comes up first in my iTunes library.) Anyway, the Emerson clone would discourage anybody from staying around for five seconds, let alone digging into the radioactive material. But the guy would never make it to the military base, because somewhere in Kansas, he'd become sexually aroused by a billboard with a slutty teenager that said "I REGRET MY ABORTION, JESUS" and start masturbating, plowing into a school bus and killing 487 people.

I didn't know any of this, and kept drinking my Scrubbing Bubbles, hoping someone as sexually attractive as said billboard model would come in for an abortion. Instead, I started wondering about the Scrubbing Bubbles, because they are anthropomorphic creatures, or objects taking on human-like qualities, and it made me wonder if Scrubbing Bubbles had human-like (or mammal-like) genitals, or if they were neuter, genderless creatures. Because Scrubbing Bubbles, at least in the commercials, appear to reproduce at a

151

great rate, in order to have such a large population. And maybe this is through mitosis or cloning or even a great Scrubbing Bubbles god that creates them, possibly sparking a Scrubbing Bubbles creationism versus evolution debate at Scrubbing Bubbles schools and among the various Scrubbing Bubbles political parties and religious organizations and sects. And maybe I can't get Scrubbing Bubbles to clean my bathroom because a large percentage of their functionality is wasted on this eternal debate.

Or maybe it's because of rampant Scrubbing Bubbles sodomy, male-on-male Scrubbing Bubbles buttsex, depraved Scrubbing Bubbles lying in wait at Scrubbing Bubbles men's rooms at truck stops, tapping their brush-bristle feet while waiting for another Scrubbing Bubble to fuck them in the ass anonymously, while they live a secret life of shame, not admitting to their wife or children or constituents (this is a senator Scrubbing Bubble we're talking about) that they secretly like to get their Scrubbing Bubble prostate stimulated by the throbbing cock of another Scrubbing Bubble penetrating their anus.

And not only does this cause the cleaner to work at a lower efficiency, but it means a Scrubbing Bubble AIDS epidemic could run rampant, killing off all of the bubbles. And I drank a can of Scrubbing Bubbles and wondered if I was actually drinking the AIDS-infected semen and santorum from millions of sodomite Scrubbing Bubbles, and if it could cross-contaminate me somehow. And my question is, can I get any coupons for free Scrubbing Bubbles?

A fan,

Dr. Alaricus Ichabod Planchet (Ret'd.)

The Mets Riot and the Butcher/Metalhead Connection

The streets flowed with destruction and the blood of civil unrest. Crazed Mets fans beheaded innocent bystanders after Jerry Seinfeld was appointed as GM. He'd replaced all the hot dogs and Cracker Jacks with decades-old ValuJet vegetarian in-flight meals as a cost-saving measure. ("What's the deal with ballpark food?") Everyone blamed meditation, the other political party, and Rudy Giuliani. F-15E Strike Eagles idled on the tarmac of Seymour Johnson Air Force Base outside of Goldsboro, South Carolina, fully fueled and loaded with Paveway II laser-guided bombs. Their pilots snorted ground-up Provigil tablets and played travel scrabble, ready at a moment's notice to fully protect the business interests of the Raytheon corporation and level the city.

I climbed from building to building on fire escapes to avoid the street mobs, dodged Molotov cocktails and cinderblocks thrown from apartment windows like a real-life version of the *Crazy Climber* arcade game, without the primitive synthesized voice yelling "Go For It!" Like the horrible Atari 2600 version, there were no giant condors or lucky balloons, either. I badly needed a drink, and maybe some motorcycle magazines with partial nudity. My stolen Netflix login went out a week ago, and I could no longer stream hot-mom yoga videos, so I was getting desperate.

A hidden little smoke shop at 179th and Grand offered an oasis full of semi-legal water pipes, overpriced international phone cards with indecipherable rates and fees, and a cooler full of long-expired drinks that hadn't been manufactured in decades. I needed caffeine, and a little riot over stadium food and signing Mark Prior as a starting pitcher wasn't going to stop me from finding some. Baseball wasn't America's third-favorite pastime anymore, after malls, sodomy, and that TV show where hillbillies ran a check cashing place and beat each other with sticks. And you can't even find a mall anymore, ever since they started tearing them down and building fake-ass city squares with a Best Buy and a Panera in the same parking lot as a Super Target.

The ethnic grocery store burned a wall of Jesus candles to protect the shopkeeper from the mobs of idiots. I found a plastic bottle of Surge, sitting in the fridge next to some containers of fishing bait and a forgotten spit cup filled with post-processed Skoal juice and phlegm. I carefully examined the top to ensure it was still factory-sealed; it looked pristine, no superglue traces or broken connectors between the cap and ring. I couldn't remember when Surge was discontinued by the Coca-Cola corporation, but it must have been decades ago. (I know it was just rebooted as a limited-edition, but that's a bullshit move. Let me have my nostalgia; it's the only thing keeping me alive at this point.) Normally,

I'd run in fear and walk another eight miles to find a more sterile source of hydration, but sometimes a man's gotta fight his thirst, and it has electrolytes. (Or maybe it doesn't.)

A redneck bruiser behind the counter pushed the carcass of an unknown animal through the whirring blade of a band saw. The fifties-era Craftsman machine buzzed through the thick flank of gristle-encrusted flesh, hesitating, sticking, smoking and burning the fat as it chipped through the meat. Every few pushes, the corpse would catch the saw blade, the band of high-speed metal locking and vibrating against a bone. The man would mutter a string of obscenities, curse Allah or God or someone, pull back the slab of meat, and try again.

I couldn't identify the mammal crushed against the saw's rip fence, but I flunked general science four times in high school and am not exactly an adept amateur zoologist. It may have been some kind of Australian kangaroo or platypus, maybe something from the recently-liquidated Detroit zoo that ended up on eBay. But watching the man slowly dismember the animal into marketable pieces gave me a strange déjà vu for another damaged meat purchase, a time when me and Warmoth Gluten argued the finer points of life.

* * *

Back in college, a metalhead by the name of Warmoth at the Kroger by the south side of campus sold me a side of broken ribs for ten cents a pound. I knew Warmoth from the local underground metal circuit, and he gave me the cheap meat hookup in exchange for dubs of obscure death metal demo tapes. I was getting a lot of freaky Japanese sex-grindcore stuff, which he was into. (I only really liked the band Sigh, when they did black metal stuff. That song "Ready For the Final War" is about perfect, but then they added a saxophone to the band and got really weird, so I don't know.)

He told me a dumb-as-dirt townie who was trying to break into the amateur MMA circuit worked part-time on the loading dock of the store, and he shattered the bones, pulverized the hanging meat in a *Rocky*-fueled training tirade. He lost in the second round of his first match at a $5 event at the abandoned K-Mart out on Walnut, a vicious knockout from a PCP-enraged Chechen foreign exchange student with lightning bolts shaved into his scalp. The match was tossed after he tested positive for angel dust in a piss test; his lawyer from the student legal center tried to contest it, saying it was a false positive because of Effexor. I didn't care about the ethics of MMA drug testing; I bought the ribs because it was better than eating ramen and generic dog food for the rest of the semester.

I would marinate the meat for ten days in a poultice of Cherry Coke, brown sugar, and cough medicine, then blaze it in a toaster oven, hoping it would taste like Chinese take-out spareribs. Two hours later, the entire student ghetto looked like nuclear winter, thick black clouds of airborne charred flesh and dextromethorphan smoke rolling across the neighborhood. They still tasted okay, after I chipped away the black embers with a crowbar and carved out the good flesh with an X-Acto knife. But I'd never get back that apartment deposit, and forget ever trying to bring home a blind date when your entire building smells like charred flesh.

Warmoth ran some mammal through a sausage machine, and I watched the large, cast-iron apparatus shit out perfect links of tubular casing filled with meat. "Dude, the other day I saw a TV show about women getting knocked up for fun, and live-blogging their abortions in high-res." The sausage machine churned and sounded like a broken vacuum cleaner as it extruded coils of meat product. "There's an app for it, even — it matches up ovulating women with dudes who don't like condoms, and lets you live-stream for free, with ads. Within a year, people are going to call you a poseur if you kill fifty kids and *don't* eat their bodies. We're strapped into a jet plummeting into a building, and nobody gives a shit."

"You're assuming society even exists. It doesn't. Maybe it died when Oswald acted alone. Maybe earlier. But clinging onto the idea that you're going to turn it around is futile. We're all fucked, and none of this matters. It's the Titanic, and there's no redheaded bitches to fuck in steerage. Get over it."

"Yeah, fuck society. Hey, you want any of these sausages? I think it's elk, or bison, or one of those animals. I hope I took the hair off before I threw it in the grinder, but I could give you like a dollar off."

"I'm good, chief." I left the meat counter and went to check out the Lunchables section. I needed to stock up, so I wouldn't have to leave the house again for a while, at least until the end of college basketball season.

* * *

Back in the present world, I set the soft drink and a bag of cheddar cheese and pretzel M&Ms on the bodega counter. The butcher hit the kill switch on the saw and pulled off his blood-drenched clear plastic goggles and elbow-length rubber gloves. Underneath his white and crimson lab coat, he wore an Anal Cunt shirt, one of those cheap insta-print things from CafePress or some other online site, the kind where the transparency in the image of a guy ass-raping a bound and gagged Japanese woman wasn't the same color of black as the shirt, making it look like a bad iron-on. It's disconcerting how many butchers are metalheads and/or into serial killers. At least it gives me something to talk to them about while I'm in line.

"How's your day been?" he said, punching keys on the ancient cash register. "Hell of a riot out there today, eh?" He slurred his words, and I initially thought he was drunk, or smoking formaldehyde, but then I saw under the three-day stubble of his shaved head a c-shaped scar, a telltale flap where a gateway to the gray matter was sawed open, probably from some traumatic brain injury sustained in a motorcycle accident or failed high-stakes maneuver in a homemade skateboarding video. I stared at the purple shape on the side of his head and wondered what happened, but didn't want to ask.

"It's a real shitstorm out there," I said. *Don't look at his scar. Don't look at his scar.* "Almost as bad as what went down after the last *Spider-Man* movie." I looked at his scar.

"Don't even get me started. When they said they were changing it so he shot his web jizz out of his asshole instead of his wrists, some fucker threw a fax machine through my front window and pissed all over my magazine rack."

Stop looking at his scar. "Fucking savages. Where do you even get a fax machine these days?"

He rubbed the scar on his head, and I looked down at the floor, but I know he saw me look at it. "It's from a craniotomy."

"The fax machine?"

"No, the scar. They had to cut open my head, excess brain pressure. Fell asleep trying to open a wall safe with a jackhammer. It was a different time. You happy?"

"Uh, sorry? Sure?" I gave him a five for the food and drink, and headed out as fast as I could. I didn't give a shit about the scar, but I did. Sometimes I wish I could right-click on everything in the world and see a properties list that explained it. I think the internet has broken me. Famous last words.

I headed back out to watch the disaster unfold. The city overflowed with the usual stupidity. Friday night riots, the big town, time to die. A group of Hare Krishna professional wrestlers pushed past me on the sidewalk, chanting and beating drums and pacing in circles outside of a macrobiotic enema store next to the bodega. They sang a Hulk Hogan song through a battery-powered PA amp that was 98% dead and distorting like an 88-pack of pencils was jammed in the speaker cones.

Everyone was throwing kitchen utensils at the passing cars. I pulled aside a guy in an orange robe who looked like a cancer-stricken Andy Dick. "Hey, what's the deal with the spatulas? What does this have to do with the Mets?" I didn't expect a straight answer, but I didn't want to get in the cross-fire if they graduated to beer steins or ninja weapons.

"It's the 24th of February! Today's the day the *Twin Peaks* TV show starts, but like for real! Do you know anything about the TRS-80? We're starting a revolution!"

"Do you mean the original Z-80-based TRS-80 or the 6809-based Color Computer? Because those are totally different things."

Someone hit me from behind with what felt like an oversized eggplant, the freakishly large ones that people bring to the county fair to win ribbons and prizes. (This was long before people started using that emoji as a dick.) I woke up later in the back of a Quizno's sandwich shop, throwing up straight mayonnaise and chunks of half-digested bacon. My discman and 72-minute CD-R of GG Allin slow jams was missing, and I couldn't find one of my shoes. I knew that in twenty minutes, an ER surgeon would be shaving my head and sawing a flap out of my skull, because karma works that way. Say your prayers, take your vitamins. Fuck the world. I am a real American.

Chili Sweats at Aerie #666

He hung out at the Eagles lodge, ran through some losing pull-tab tickets and drank Manhattans made with Gem Clear and Heinz cocktail sauce, complaining about how the Mexicans blew up Tower 7 and women's lib was responsible for the Brylcreem shortage. He looked like a deformed Howard Hughes, without the money to bang out Hollywood whores and live in the top ten floors of an expensive hotel, only making a few bucks a week from a low-end day job as an hourly shoe salesman at the Big R farm store south of town.

He was supposed to bowl in a tournament, but he couldn't stand up anymore. Jimmy Three Tits would take his place, and roll a 74 with a women's dayglo-pink six-pound ball, just so the other guys would call him a lady-boy in the locker room, something he secretly enjoyed. But bizarro Howard stayed slumped at the bar, sucking down his last twelve dollars on cheap drinks.

"Got the chili sweats something fierce," he told the bartender. "I don't think I'm going to make it to a toilet." He leaned over and started shitting his pants at the bar, screaming "avenge me! AVENGE ME!" but nobody knew the movie reference, because it hadn't been remade in the last six months.

47 years before, Walter Mondale stood in the ballroom of the once-great art deco aerie hall, giving a two-hour speech on the importance of trade unions. Now, the addled alcoholic's bowels ran down his pant legs, dumping hot chili shit onto the waxed wood floor.

Fuck Beets

Fat Mike called me three times in the middle of the night, leaving twenty-minute-long rambling messages on my machine which I promptly deleted without screening. After every debt collector in the free world started calling my number ten times a day to extort the unpaid balance on a US West bill for some random idiot — and US West hadn't existed in like a decade — I started turning off my ringer and muting the answering machine before I chugged my evening bottle of Robitussin. The night prior, I'd passed out in the bathtub reading a waterlogged issue of *Penthouse* so old, the women still had bush. The second I turned back on the phone the next morning, it started ringing immediately.

I put him on speaker while I crushed up enough Allegra-D tablets to live. This was springtime in New York, and even though New York had like one gnarly, leafless tree per square mile, they had all deposited a record amount of pollen directly into my lungs and eyes. I don't know how that works. Karma, maybe. I am a horrible person. I fully deserve every bad thing that happens to me.

"God damn it why aren't you answering your phone? It's not like you're out getting pussy. I could be here with six German porn stars and you've got your fucking phone unplugged. You need to have that shit on at all times. It's not like they charge you to have the phone on the hook."

"Hello to you too." I looked at my watch and started the algebraic equation of how long it would take me to shit/shower/shave, the duration of the commute to Manhattan, how many hours he would keep me on the phone talking about some fucking European release of a Venom cassette, and how late I could show up at the office and still sneak out at five. It wasn't looking great. Maybe I'd skip shaving. "So what's your major malfunction?"

"FUCK BEETS, MOTHERFUCKER!" His screaming sounded like some vintage 80s lo-fi hate-core band recorded on a Radio Shack tape deck in the middle of the woods because they spent all of Roadrunner Records' money on a black Corvette and an entire truck stop of speed. "FUCK BEETS! FUCK BEETS IN THE ASS AND MOUTH AND MAKE YOUR MOTHER WATCH! DID YOU EVEN LISTEN TO MY MESSAGES?"

"No, I didn't listen to them. What's your problem with the Beats? Did you find out Alfred Ginsburg was a card-carrying NAMBLA member?"

"Not *the* beats — beets. Two e's. I mean, fuck Ginsburg, but more importantly, fuck beets!"

"I didn't even think they had vegetables out there yet. One time you had your mom make us a steak salad, and it was just chunks of meat and croutons in a plastic rubbermaid bowl, drenched in a gallon of ranch."

"It had crispy onions too. Onions are a vegetable! Anyway, fuck that — I was reading this book about secrets — I thought it would have some pictures of tits, like Victoria's Secret — but it's shit like the KFC recipe and that hidden place at Disneyland that serves booze, like anyone gives a fuck. There was a big section on food additives and secret sauces, and they said that the Illuminati is trying to get Coca-Cola to switch from using real sugar to some fuckin' hippy yo-yo beet juice sugar so they can save like a penny per year or some shit."

"How old is that book? They switched to high fructose corn syrup decades ago. It's why Pepsi tastes like mouthwash now."

"FUCK BEETS! IF I WANTED TO EAT VEGETABLES I'D MOVE TO SOME FUCKING COMMUNE WHERE THE CHICKS DON'T SHAVE THEIR PITS AND DO BUTT STUFF! FUCK THAT! FUCK CORN! FUCK BEETS! FUCK ALL FRUITS AND VEGETABLES! FUCK EVERYTHING!"

Fat Mike had a tendency to become unhinged at tangental items that didn't matter whatsoever, spending weeks or even months griping about the inconsequential, usually based on headlines of articles he didn't even read on completely unreliable conspiracy web sites. One recent rant was about the expansion of the Panama Canal; he acted like the two summers he spent trying to get his dick sucked in a 14-foot boat made him an authority on the construction of international waterways. That whole campaign started because of the Van Halen song "Panama" and ended with him mailing bags of shit to Manuel Noriega in the Federal Correction Institute in Miami, at which point a postal inspector showed up at Fat Mike's mom's house and told him to stop sending human feces through the federal mails. (And yes, they somehow knew it was human fecal matter and not animal. Either it was that obvious that Fat Mike eats Taco Bell four times a day, or some federal crime lab technician in Maryland had a really bad day of work.)

"God DAMN it. Oh man, I forgot to tell you. I found the Diet Pepsi Frito pie chick on Facebook!" Fat Mike had a horrible habit of referring to people by event or scenario instead of name. This one was a woman he wanted to fuck twenty years ago, who was in the lesbian film studies class he took to get laid. I don't remember where Diet Pepsi or Frito pie came into account, but I instantly knew who he was talking about, so I guess his derogatory system does work.

"Wonderful. Did you literally search on 'diet pepsi frito pie' or did you remember her last name?"

"Dude, she's gone full lez. She's a cop now, in some shit-kicker one-sheriff town like Logansport or Peru or something, one of those villages with only one gas station that sells porno and anal lube to truckers."

"Just because she's a police officer doesn't mean she's a lesbian. You're just pissed she wouldn't suck your dick."

"I'm not talking about like a Heather Locklear cop, like on that show with the *Star Wars* dude with the fake wig. I mean like a full-on short-hair cop. I'm sort of into it, actually."

"I thought you hated cops. You've been arrested for jerking off at Big R like nine times."

"Their slogan is 'You'll Love What's In Store' — if that's not a clear invitation to bust a load while you're scoping out a cashier and looking at livestock gear, I don't know what is. Anyway, they're never going to catch me again. I'm like the Zodiac Killer of jerking off in department stores." I had a sudden mind-bleach-required vision of Ted Cruz belting one out in the housewares section of a K-Mart, and wondered if I could use the ensuing PTSD as a medical requirement for euthanasia medication in Oregon.

"I hope that means you're going to start mailing your jizz rags to San Francisco newspapers."

"Oh man, speaking of jerking off in department stores, the other day I dropped a load at the Super Target, and fell asleep driving home from the mall. I dreamed I got a blowjob from a conjoined twin. It was that chick — or those chicks, whatever — from the *Teen Conjoined Twin Moms* show, with one lower body, and two heads. Just one of the mouths sucked my dick. The right mouth was eating a pizza and talking on the phone to her tax attorney. Maybe that's only half a blowjob. And she didn't finish, so it was only a quarter-job."

"Wait, did they each have to file a 1040, or do they file jointly? Because that would suck from a dependency point of view if they could only take one standard deduction, especially since they probably aren't having kids."

"How the fuck do I know how the bitch filed her taxes? I was getting a blow job. I'm not H&R fucking Block. Anyway, I crashed my mom's car into a brick wall by that Mennonite church where the chicks don't shave their legs. Totally fucked up the hood and front of the car, and probably did something to the church, but fuck them anyway. Worst of all, I didn't even get to jizz down that bitch's left throat."

I only passively listened to Fat Mike's phone bitch-fest, while I read an old *Car Craft* magazine about big block Chevy performance tips. I picked at a scab on my knee from trying to jump a graveyard fence while taking a shortcut to a 7-Eleven that sold Mountain Dew Slurpees and had no cameras. I drizzled some peroxide on the wound from a bottle that came with my apartment, and watched the pus foam like a vinegar and baking soda volcano from a grade school science fair.

"Hey man, I just found out my old roommate got a job as a professional wrestler," he said. "He still owes me half the rent for the rest of of that lease. Took my Sega Genesis, too, the *Sonic* game, the CD drive, and everything. He was going to wire me some money for his share until we could find a sublet, but nobody answered the ads...."

"Wait, weren't those the flyers that said 'in search of sluts with huge tits into Satanism who will pay all my rent and suck my dick' and had a bunch of pictures of King Diamond and zombie movies all over them, and the manager at Kroger gave you a lifetime ban for putting them up next to the check cashing counter?"

"Yeah! FUCK CENSORSHIP! I know I would have gotten a ton of replies on those ads, too."

About the roommate — I'd heard the story before, a thousand times, at least once a week since it happened. His name was Axl, and he always smelled like bootleg Marlboros and burning motor oil. He drove an El Camino with no mufflers, a naked slut wrapped in a confederate flag painted on the tailgate, her body pocked with rust holes that looked like impetigo sores. His day job involved loading trucks at a dildo factory on the edge of town, but he always talked about becoming a pro rassler. He was so stupid, he didn't even know wrestling was fake. When he wasn't forklifting crates of buttplugs onto semi trucks, he practiced hitting himself in the head with a chair and yelling promos into the security camera in the break room.

"I found that piece of shit online last week, at this site that's like the IMDB of amateur wrestling. He only had three matches, in this promotion that operated in an abandoned Target outside Orlando. He'd get the shit beat out of him by a guy who dressed up in a sombrero and glue-on mustache and called himself The Mexican. The dude's closing move was 'The Fourth Meal.'"

"That promoter's lucky he didn't get a cease and desist from Yum! Brands, the parent company of Taco Bell. They just shut down the director of that porn movie *Kentucky Fucked Chicks*."

"Maybe they did get shut down. All I know is Ax-hole got hooked on heroin and moved to Vegas to do gay porn. He gets topped by some guy in a Liberace costume and probably makes fifty bucks a day. You can't even get the buffet at Circus Circus for that anymore. And they don't give you steak, either, those pricks. That fucker can rot in hell."

"At least you got to use his spare room for overflow comic storage before you had to move back to your mom's house."

"Speaking of comics, are you going to get the new *X-Men*? It comes out today."

"I haven't read comic books in twenty years. I couldn't name you three of the X-Men if I had a poster in front of me. I don't even know for sure that it's a crime-fighting team. For all I know, it could be a dance troupe." (This was years before Marvel did make an off-Broadway dance troupe based on the X-Men characters. I think they all play drums like that *Stomp* musical. Well, maybe the bald dude in the wheelchair doesn't.)

"Well, get it. Go get it immediately. They're rebooting the Dark Phoenix Saga, but it's all in 3-D and they made Jean Grey a lesbian and all the issues are being printed with six different covers in different bags and sleeves so you have to buy every copy 24 times. It's going to be awesome."

"Dude. I've gotta go to work."

"Fine, be a dumb ass. FUCK BEETS."

The Twilight Be- tween Sleep and Death

The tallest building on main street was a dozen stories high, a nursing home for aging clowns and sonogram technicians, the result of a farm union merger gone insane. This was a town that did not believe in vertical construction, the twentieth century, or the number pi. They once passed a law banning computers because you could type 7734 into a calculator and flip it over to say HELL. And every time it snowed, the town paper had a Pearl Harbor-sized headline about how global warming was bullshit. I'd be lucky to find anyone willing to treat my latest mystery stomach ailment without mentioning Jesus at least five times per sentence.

I eventually stumbled across a retired x-ray tech on Craigslist who would scan my abdomen for cash on the down-low. After a week of phone tag, we made plans for the procedure. I had to meet him at his retirement home and bring soup, lube, and something to clean his ceiling fan, like an extended-reach feather duster or one of those Swiffer sweepers with a telescopic arm attachment. Also the soup had to be low sodium, which was a bitch to find, since soup is basically 90% salt at this point.

The retired geezer's apartment looked like the set to a prewar Howard Hawks film about a destitute hoarder, but with more dust. The white-haired man wheeled out a Philips EPIQ 7 ultrasound rig and offered to image up my wang and email the scans to potential dates, the latest craze with the younger kids — we've all had that typical first-date scenario where you can't get her pants off until she knows if you have a pre-existing urinary tract condition. I stuck with the full abdomen series, no funny business. He promised me full twilight anesthesia and a disc of the data in his cash price, plus a discount code for a free 100 hours of CompuServe. His DVD-ROM burner put a trialware Windows program and a bunch of bullshit auto-run toolbars filled with online poker ads on each CD, but you can download the free version of OsiriX for the Mac and easily manipulate the DICOM images to post them online.

The amateur radiologist squirted a pint of cold ultrasound transmission gel on my stomach. It felt like icy jism, a slippery, frothy load of aqueous conductor. "Doppler transmission of the gods, the wrath of sound and fury. Won't hurt one bit..." He wore camo scrubs, desert brown and tan fatigue colors instead of the usual bright aquamarine. I gazed at the brown liver spots on his faded, baggy skin, and counted backwards from a thousand while the Demerol flowed through my veins. The tech babbled on about his life while the meds took hold. "Bought a cargo crane back in '87, got loaded on Bacardi and tried to drive the thing to Pittsburgh. Lots of crazy Penguins hockey fans would pay top dollar for a crane ride." He put on the second Gorgoroth album, and I heard the first few seconds of "En stram lukt av kristent blod" (A Rank Smell of Christian Blood) echo through the improvised medical sleep before I lost consciousness.

In the twilight between sleep and death, I flirted with the idea of visualizing a passage from the asteroid back to the earth, a conduit leading from one celestial body to another, and the lucid-dream thought would magically make it happen. Would the ability to dream of one reality prevent the ability to tunnel into another dream state, another world? Would the other planet's existence be an extension of his current dream, or would his mind power alone burrow into another consciousness, another plane of existence, or even another person's dream? I couldn't focus on the tunnel, couldn't keep it in mind for long enough for it to materialize. It seemed too simple, too obvious, thinking of a time-shaft from one world to another and hoping it would mystically open. Maybe my lack of belief prevented the magical placebo effect he needed to make it work.

The sky didn't grow dark in my dream; it stayed a perpetual, hazy gray. I couldn't recall from Astronomy 101 if a small planetary body, like a moon or asteroid only a few miles across would have the same day/night characteristics of a large planet. I remembered that stupid Bruce Willis movie got it wrong, but that wasn't exactly a scientific textbook — Ben Affleck said there were 54 states in the Union, and Billy Bong Thornton mentioned the Civil War happening in 1947. I couldn't do the math, if the asteroid was orbiting or did orbit another planet, if it had days or nights, or if its sky would change. All I could remember from trig class was SOH CAH TOA, and a substitute teacher who never wore a bra. I started at the twilight, until it finally blended into the ambient light of the half-lit retirement home. The crazed and senile sonogram technician was trying to snort enough Viagra to jerk off to my prone body while squirting a tube of ultrasound gel up his asshole. I got my CD-ROM, and left quickly.

* * *

A distant memory, the insane asylum was torn down in the era between quality printed maps and the internet surveillance state aerial images of every square inch of the country, meaning I could not find any imagery of it anywhere. The county home stood next the river, a massive gothic structure built a century before to hold invalids, poor, orphans, and the insane. When I was a kid, I used to hop inner tubes with the other neighborhood juvenile delinquents, and float past the home, trying to spot a terminal psych case in captivity. I hoped to catch a fleeting glimpse of a real life Ed Gein type, a terminally insane murderer working a Siberian forced labor gig, a make-busy thing like clearing brush or moving the same pile of cinderblocks from one side of the barbed wire compound to the other. I obsessed over serial killers, freak shows, the deformed, depraved, and damaged. That county home was my only gateway in real life to seeing the things I found in true crime books and the *Weekly World News* tales of horror.

A decade later, they sprung loose all of the crazies, one of those get-rid-of-big-government plans: save the county a few bucks by dropping off all of the incurable Charlie Mansons at the Amtrak station downtown with a twenty dollar bill and a five-day bus pass. (I don't remember if this was a Reagan policy, or if the local government was furiously circle-jerking to Reagan and came up with the legislation themselves.) Never mind that they'd run rampant, smoking angel dust and chopping kids into lunchmeat; the next round of politicians would inherit the problem. Who cares if the I-got-mine government dismantling turned the entire county into an insane asylum.

The unused building sat empty, abandoned, covered in graffiti, a monument to the tragedy of the past. Hipster urban explorer types broke out the windows and tagged the limestone walls. Fires flickered inside from squatters and addicts looking for a place to fix. The county put up signs and razor wire, but that never stops anybody. It became a free-for-all, part heroin shooting gallery, part outdoor toilet, a ghost of its former self. A decade later, some junkies trying to cook dope would burn it to the ground. They bulldozed the remains, planted grass, and now nothing remains.

* * *

Back in the late Seventies, they locked a guy in there on an insanity plea, for the Frances Farmer treatment, wet sheets and some icepick scrapey-scrape. They'd later flip his diagnosis back to sane — treatment complete, cured— and fry him in the electric chair. He was a spree killer who thought he was immune to police bullets because he drank a lot of milk and took calcium supplements, and briefly got some news cycles, before Tito Jackson released that concept album about fucking a dead dog in the parking lot of a K-Mart. (It's actually an overlooked classic, if you can find a copy. Michael Schenker played guitar on two tracks, and it was produced by Eddie Kramer, with Bob Ludwig handling the CD mastering.)

While the ultimate cop killer warrior got his daily beatdown, a little kid rode his bike in circles around the insane asylum, muttering something about having to find his parents, when all of the workers knew they got killed in a freak LSD lab explosion accident back in 1977. "I am the cheese! I am the full-fat, made in Wisconsin, clog-your-fat-arteries cheese!" he chanted, nobody listening to his madness. So many video games had sampled catch phrases played after you decapitate a hooker, nobody could remember if this was a quote from a DeNiro movie or an episode of *Chico and the Man*.

A minimum-wage staffer injected the brat with Thorazine and the pounded-out dust of Flintstones chewables mixed with Gatorade to stop any latent thoughts, and hoped for the best. As long as the kid didn't see any long-dead twins or start writing REDRUM on the mirrors and walls in his blood, everything would be golden. No matter what happened, the state gave the facility $377 a month for his care. They could lock him in a room in the ancient dungeon with a hundred other feral kids for a dollar a day, provided the government kept sending them free cheese. You can make almost anything out of government cheese if you have enough slave labor to pound it into patties, soups, bread dough, and confinement loaf.

"Lobotomy! Lobotomy!" An addled speed freak on work release tapped away Ramones songs with his ball-peen hammer and icepick on the brain-scrape assembly line out at the old power building of the asylum. Fatbody guards strapped down miscreant youth to the conveyor belt and beat them senseless, while Johnny Gluesniffer scraped the steel tool through their occipital lobes, slicing apart any hostility and rage. "Now I guess you'll have to tell 'em / that you've got no cerebellum," he said erroneously. (He quoted the song correctly, but it was medically inaccurate. While Douglas Glenn Colvin may have been an excellent lyricist, he was not a medical doctor. In a leukotomy, the metal prod actually slices through a prefrontal lobe of the cerebrum, not the area around the brain stem. Still a great tune, though.)

* * *

A quick phone scan produced a list of spree killers on wikipedia, but not the milk-bulletproof guy. I got side-tracked trying to remember the name of that Australian guy that went postal on a resort in Tasmania or Australia or whatever. False flag, Duane would tell me, conspiracy theory on gun ownership. I just remember he got a pension for being mentally retarded — the Australian guy, not Duane. Duane didn't get anything for his low IQ, except a lot of grief and many inane ideas on how the UN was making recreational laxatives mandatory.

Driving, driving to a mall, the answer for everything twenty years ago, and now they don't even have malls, but I drove in circles anyway, like an idiot. A guy in a beaten econobox pulled next to me, matching my speed. I probably unknowingly passed through some down-low cruising area, a lover's lane for anonymous sodomites. He drove a shit-brown AMC Pacer, and wore a pink and baby blue short-sleeved button-up shirt with a pocket full of pens like a high school math teacher, his bad comb-over twisted apart by the wind from the hatchback's giant windows, a flailing frond of hair whipping in the turbulence.

"HASBRO NORWOOD HAS CORNERED THE MARKET ON REUSABLE ADULT DIAPERS! LET ME SELL YOU A VOWEL!" He kept shouting and honking his horn, not slowing down as we approached the humpback railroad crossing. I watched him keep on the gas, ramming through the gate and colliding into a passing Burlington Northern freight train, demolishing the squat bug-like car, its substandard fuel tank exploding like a terrorist bomb, taking out five other passing automobiles and two hopper cars full of fertilizer. It would take emergency response teams a week to contain the scene, put out the flames, and scrape all of the pieces of the corpses out of the gravel.

I flipped a 27-point turn in the intersection of the five-lane highways and drove south, parallel to the tracks, driving past the wreckage of the miles-long train and hoping to eventually find the end and get to the other side. I did the same thing at least once a week, trying to beat a hundred-car traffic divider like a East German fighting a moving version of the Berlin wall. The landscape on either side was nothingness, prairies flattened by tornado after tornado, only grass-covered concrete blocks remaining of basement-less crawl space foundations where single-wide trailers were plucked from the ground and thrown thousands of yards away with the force of a vengeful old testament god. Tornado alley? More like tornado highway.

Past the remains of the drive-through movie theater, long ago shuttered and turned into a weekend flea market of car stereos stolen by meth addicts and useless hillbilly trinkets drop-shipped in bulk from China, a set of crossing gates stood open, a second train a solid five seconds away from me. I hung a big left at top speed and hopped over the tracks just as the red lights fired up and the black and white arms descended to block traffic. Now five miles south of where I wanted to be, I hung another left and headed back north.

I can't watch railroad cars pass by anymore — childhood trauma, PTSD, or maybe epilepsy, induced by the flashing bits of metal on the edge of each car. I contemplated how many baby aspirin I'd have to pack into the cavities of my ventricles to become completely immune to heart attacks. Every brand of aspirin is now propaganda for Jesus, the name of some saint or Judeo-Christian corporation with an agenda to kill us all. The same people that make your kid's organic vegan diapers also brewed up every gallon of napalm we dropped on the 'Cong back in the day. It's all about money.

The Pink Floyd bootleg droned on, one of the early ones when Syd was still trippin' balls and pushing the mod noise into interstellar overdrive. It was a bootleg from some forgotten British channel, or maybe it was from Hong Kong — Bruce Lee narrated the whole thing, doing flying kicks in the air. It was on a LaserDisc I bought from a freaky Anime place deep in the village, a basement full of oddball PAL tapes of Romanian whores getting fucked by octopuses. It was all overpriced, but I still spent a lot of time there. I had nothing better to do, except flip through the used section and wait to die.

About the Author

Jon Konrath is an American author born in 1971. He grew up in Indiana and studied computer science and English at Indiana University. After college, he worked as a software developer and technical writer, but eventually turned his attention to writing fiction.

Konrath is the author of several books, including *Rumored to Exist*, *Thunderbird*, and *The Earworm Inception*. His writing is known for its unique blend of humor, absurdism, and surrealism, often blurring the lines between reality and fantasy.

In addition to writing, Konrath is also an accomplished photographer. He currently resides in California. He has been blogging at rumored.com since 1997.